Just a Bit Twisted

(Straight Guys Book 1)

Alessandra Hazard

ISBN: 9781075736568

This book contains explicit M/M content and graphic language. For mature audiences only.

Table of Contents

Chapter One....................6

Chapter Two....................10

Chapter Three....................16

Chapter Four....................27

Chapter Five....................38

Chapter Six....................43

Chapter Seven....................48

Chapter Eight....................64

Chapter Nine....................69

Chapter Ten....................74

Chapter Eleven....................83

Chapter Twelve....................89

Chapter Thirteen....................96

Chapter Fourteen....................102

Chapter Fifteen....................112

Chapter Sixteen....................117

Chapter Seventeen 121
Chapter Eighteen 129
Chapter Nineteen 135
Chapter Twenty 139
Chapter Twenty-One 145
Chapter Twenty-Two 149
Chapter Twenty-Three 155
Excerpt from Just a Bit Obsessed 159
About the Author 165

Just a Bit Twisted

Chapter One

Mrs. Hawkins was going to kill him.

Shawn glanced at his watch and grimaced. It was one in the morning already; he had promised Mrs. Hawkins he wouldn't come home later than midnight.

Bracing himself, he opened the door as quietly as he could. Emily was a light sleeper.

Shawn closed the door, wincing when it creaked.

Dammit.

"Mr. Wyatt?" Mrs. Hawkins said, rubbing her eyes and sitting up on the couch.

Shawn glanced at the twins, but they didn't seem to have woken up.

Their babysitter was frowning deeply, an unhappy look on her face.

"I'm sorry," Shawn said before she could say anything. "I'm really, really sorry. It won't happen again, I swear. I couldn't get back sooner. It was a slow night, and I didn't get a lot of tips. I didn't have enough money to pay you for this week, so I ended up staying until I did."

Mrs. Hawkins's lips pursed.

She sighed. "Mr. Wyatt—Shawn. I understand your situation—it's the only reason I'm still here—but you must understand mine, as well. I have a family, too, but I spend up to fifteen hours a day here, looking after two energetic four-year-olds. You don't pay me enough for that."

"I'll find another job," Shawn said quickly, trying to squash down the panic rising in his chest. "I'll find a better job and I'll pay you more."

She sighed again, shaking her head. "That's what you said last month, Shawn." She looked at the girls. "I admire your dedication, but it can't go on like that. You're just twenty. You deserve better. They deserve better, too. Why don't you find them a good family?"

"No," he said, his voice hard. "They already have a family. They have me."

"They barely see you. They ask about you all the time. They miss you."

Shawn looked down at the girls. Emily and Bee slept curled into each other, their chubby cheeks almost touching.

A lump formed in his throat. "I miss them, too." He looked at Mrs. Hawkins. "Please. I'll find a solution. It really won't happen again." Fishing his wallet out of his back pocket, he gave her all the money he had. "Here, take this."

She shook her head but accepted the money. "Think about what I said, Shawn," she said before taking her purse and leaving.

Shawn locked the door and returned to his sisters. He knelt down beside the bed, rested his chin on the mattress, and stared at the twins.

The dim light made their platinum blond hair seem almost golden. They looked like little angels.

Shawn closed his eyes. God, he was so tired, but sleep was the last thing on his mind. He didn't need to open the fridge to know they were out of groceries: he knew how long it took them to run out. They would have nothing to eat the day after tomorrow.

Desperation clawed up his throat. Then came resentment and anger.

Shawn shook them off. Being angry with his parents for having numerous debts, dying and leaving them penniless was useless. He couldn't afford to waste time. He needed money. Now.

But how? He already worked two jobs.

"Shawn?"

Shawn opened his eyes. One of the girls was no longer asleep. A surge of panic coursed through him when he realized he could no longer tell them apart. Was it Emily or Bee?

"Baby?" he croaked out through the lump in his throat.

The little girl sat up slowly, careful not to wake up her sister, and Shawn breathed out. It was Emily: she was more mature and considerate than Bee, who was a clueless ball of energy.

Emily reached out to him, and Shawn lifted her into his arms. "Hey, princess," he whispered, kissing her on the temple and breathing in her sweet scent.

"You're home," Emily said, wrapping her little arms around his neck. "Missed you."

"Me, too," Shawn murmured, stroking her back. *I'm sorry.* "Did you have fun while I was out?"

Emily nodded. "We played a lot, but the Hawk didn't let us go outside!"

"Don't call Mrs. Hawkins that." Though he had to suppress a smile. "Anything else?"

"A big man came after breakfast. He had a letter for you, but the Hawk didn't let us touch it."

"A letter, huh?" Shawn got to his feet, cradling Emily to his chest, and walked to his desk. "Let's see."

He picked up the envelope and returned to the bedside lamp. He squinted at it and his stomach dropped when he saw who it was from.

"What is it?" Emily asked.

Shawn opened the envelope, pulled out the piece of paper inside and started to read.

"…unacceptable grades…" "…upon failure of improvement…" "…scholarship will be terminated unless the student achieves…"

The paper dropped from his fingers to the floor and he didn't notice.

"Shawn? Something bad happened?"

He looked down at Emily's wide blue eyes and forced a smile. "No, pumpkin. Everything is fine." He buried his face in her hair and closed his eyes.

When it rained, it poured.

Chapter Two

"Something wrong?" said a familiar voice before an arm was slung around Shawn's shoulders.

Shawn glanced at Christian, but kept walking. Their next class was going to start in ten minutes and it was one he couldn't be late for. "Nothing."

"Bullshit. Spill." His friend's dark brown eyes were fixed on him curiously.

Shawn shrugged. "I'm broke. And on top of that, they're going to terminate my scholarship if I don't improve my grades in three classes."

Christian frowned. "I thought you already talked to Bates and Summers and explained your situation."

Sighing, Shawn raked a hand through his hair. "Yeah. But there's also Fluid Mechanics."

Christian grimaced. "Rutledge."

"Yep," Shawn said miserably.

The school's youngest tenured professor, Derek Rutledge had the nickname "Professor Asshole" for a reason. Strict and harsh, he set impossibly high standards for students and despised those who failed to achieve them. He didn't tolerate "laziness." And since Shawn missed too many of his lectures and often didn't have time to complete his assignments, he was probably one of Rutledge's least favorite students—if the man even had favorite students.

The chances of Rutledge cutting him some slack were nonexistent. Rutledge didn't cut anyone any slack. His demands bordered on ridiculous, but in the board's eyes Rutledge could do no wrong, since he garnered a lot of research grants—like, *a lot*. Shawn had to give Rutledge credit—one didn't become such a highly respected researcher by the age of thirty-three if one wasn't incredibly intelligent—but it didn't change the fact that the guy was a total asshole.

"What are you going to do?" Christian said.

"No idea." Shawn made his way to their usual seats at the front of the lecture hall: Rutledge had ordered him and Christian to sit there all the time after he had caught them talking during his class. Shawn sat down and sighed. "What should I do?"

"I wish I could help you." Christian dropped into a seat next to him. "But you know I'm a bit tight on the money, too."

Shawn nodded. Christian lived at his grandmother's and helped her as much as he could. His parents worked in another country and weren't much of a help.

"What about your aunt?" Christian said. "I thought she used to help you out when things got tough."

Shawn paused and gave him a look. "She died last year, Chris. I told you that."

Christian's face flushed bright red. "Shit, I'm sorry—I don't know how I—"

Shawn shook his head. "Forget it." It wasn't that Christian didn't care; he was just very sociable and had more friends than Shawn had acquaintances. No wonder it had slipped out of his mind.

"What about your cousin—Sage?" Christian smiled sheepishly. "See, I'm not completely hopeless! I remember him!"

Shawn laughed. "You are hopeless. He just recently got out of prison, and he needs to sort out his life. He doesn't need my problems on top of his own. Anyway, I wasn't asking about money. I meant Professor Rutledge. If I don't get good grades in his class, I'll lose the scholarship and will have to drop out."

Though sometimes Shawn wondered if it would be better to drop out: if he didn't have school to attend, it would improve his chances of finding a half-decent job. Except a college degree would increase his chances of finding a well-paid job and giving Emily and Bee everything they needed as they grew up.

"Actually," Christian said suddenly. "I've heard an interesting rumor about Rutledge."

"What rumor?"

Christian glanced around, as though to make sure no one could hear them, before leaning in and murmuring into Shawn's ear, "Tucker says Professor Rutledge has a weakness for pretty boys."

Shawn blinked. "No way. He was just messing with you!"

"Nope, he was dead serious. Apparently someone

saw Rutledge with a young guy all over him."

Shawn chuckled, shaking his head. "Even if it's true, what does it have to do with me?"

Christian gave him a pointed look.

Shawn opened his mouth, closed it, and then opened it again. "You've got to be kidding me."

Christian wiggled his eyebrows. "Tucker says Rutledge has a thing for blonds."

"Unlucky for you, then."

Smiling, Christian ran a hand through his messy brown hair. "Pfft. If I wanted to, it wouldn't matter. But you've got it easy, blondie. Come on, man, it's a perfect solution!"

Shawn gave him a pinched look. "There's a tiny problem, though. I'm straight."

His friend didn't look fazed; he actually had the nerve to laugh. "So what? I'm not telling you to take it up the ass. Though it can actually feel very, very good if the other guy knows what he's doing." Christian grinned, and Shawn snorted. Christian was bisexual and had no problem admitting his love for cock.

"Chris—"

"I'm just saying you can be all flirty and shit without actually doing anything with him, you know? You've got the looks. I mean—you're not my type, but I'm not blind. You're hot. Easily the hottest guy in school."

"You aren't exactly an ugly duckling, either." Everyone loved Christian. He might not be classically handsome, but practically everyone found him attractive. Christian was hard to look away from.

Shawn might be straight, but even he sometimes stopped and stared when his friend smiled.

Christian winked. "Definitely not an ugly duckling, but I ain't as pretty as you, princess."

"Oh, I'll show you, princess!" Shawn got him into a headlock, both of them laughing.

"Mr. Wyatt, Mr. Ashford, if you are quite done?" came a cold voice from behind them.

Shawn froze before letting go of his friend and straightening up. He didn't dare look at Rutledge as the man moved past them to his desk. The lecture hall suddenly became quiet.

"Fuck," Christian whispered.

Shawn bit his lip hard and stole a glance at the professor. Rutledge's dark eyes were fixed on Christian, his dark brows furrowed and his lips pursed in displeasure. Even when he wasn't unhappy with someone, Professor Rutledge's gaze could make anyone squirm. When he actually *was* unhappy, no one wanted to be on the receiving end of his heavy stares. Shawn thought he looked like a hawk, ready to swoop down and catch its prey.

Rutledge's eyes moved from Christian to him. If possible, he looked even more displeased now, a muscle pulsing in his cheek. Shawn's stomach tightened into a knot. He wet his dry lips and tried to look as respectful as possible, forcing himself to meet the professor's eyes firmly. He wasn't a coward, dammit. Rutledge was just a man.

Rutledge's lips thinned. "Mr. Wyatt," he said quietly.

Shawn swallowed convulsively. There was something about Rutledge's voice that made it more menacing the quieter it got. "Yes, Professor?"

"If you and Mr. Ashford are not interested in what I am here to teach, you may leave."

Looking at the man's hard expression, Shawn suddenly remembered Christian's advice and nearly laughed out loud—so ridiculous it was.

"No, sir. I mean, we're very interested." When not a single muscle moved on Rutledge's face, Shawn added, "Actually, I wanted to talk to you after class about my grades."

Rutledge looked at him for a few moments before offering a cool response, "I don't have office hours today." He sat down behind his desk and started his lecture.

Shawn looked at him blankly, unsure what Rutledge's answer was supposed to mean. Was that yes or no? As in, "I don't have office hours, so you may come" or "I don't have office hours, so you can't"?

Great. Fantastic.

Chapter Three

The door to Professor Rutledge's office was dark and very shiny.

Shawn stared at it, trying to ignore the uneasy feeling in his gut. His palms were beginning to sweat, so he wiped them against his jeans.

Don't be ridiculous, he told himself. Rutledge was just a man, not a monster. The worst thing the guy could do was say no. He would just talk to him, explain his situation and hope Rutledge wasn't the asshole everyone thought he was.

"Did you want something, Mr. Wyatt?" a smooth, low voice said.

Shawn nearly jumped. Turning around, he tried to find something to say.

"Mr. Wyatt?" Rutledge was frowning, a crease between his eyebrows.

"I wanted to talk to you, sir."

"It's not an office hour," Rutledge said, unlocking his office and going inside. He didn't swing the door shut behind him, and Shawn hesitated, unsure if he was meant to follow him inside. Rutledge sat down behind his massive desk and turned on his computer.

"I don't have all day, Wyatt," he said without looking at him.

Shawn entered the room hurriedly. He closed the door, walked to the desk and stopped. He looked around, but there wasn't much to look at.

"Well?"

Shawn forced himself to look at the other man.

Rutledge was studying him with a hint of impatience.

Shawn gripped the back of the chair in front of him. "As I said, I wanted to talk about my grades."

Rutledge's lips pressed into a thin line. "I'm not certain what there is to talk about. I don't give second chances to students who don't deserve them. You don't bother to attend most of my lectures, the quality of your coursework is abysmal, and now you want a passing grade. The policy concerning class attendance is clearly stated on the class syllabus; students should read this policy carefully and should plan on complying with it. Frankly, I'm surprised you're a scholarship student. If you're worried about your scholarship, I'm afraid the only thing you can do is drop the class."

"I can't drop your class—it's a co-requisite for another class I'm currently taking and I can't drop both without losing my scholarship. So I can't fail your class and I can't drop it. I need a passing grade, sir."

The look Rutledge gave him was unimpressed. "You can blame only yourself, Wyatt. You don't deserve a better grade."

"Your attendance, assignments, class participation, and test grades have been below expectations for the course. If you came here to tell me some sob story and beg me for a better grade, save your breath. I've heard it all: sick elderly mothers, little children to look after, working three jobs, and so forth. If you can't or don't want to study and learn, do both of us a favor: stop wasting our time and drop out of college."

Shawn's heart sank. A part of him had hoped Rutledge would take pity on him if he told him about his situation and let him turn in his assignments late. But apparently, Rutledge didn't care and didn't want to listen to "sob stories."

Shawn's jaw tightened. His pride urged him to turn around and leave, but he couldn't. He couldn't lose the scholarship. His sisters depended on him.

Suddenly, he remembered Christian's ridiculous advice.

...says Professor Rutledge has a weakness for pretty boys... I'm just saying you can be all flirty and shit without actually doing anything with him...

"Mr. Wyatt?"

Shawn flinched, flushed, and looked back at the man.

"What are you still doing in my office? You're dismissed."

Looking at Rutledge's hard expression, Shawn couldn't for the life of him imagine flirting with him. "Flirting" and "Professor Rutledge" shouldn't even be mentioned in the same sentence, period. And Shawn didn't have much experience with flirting, anyway: the few girls he'd had sex with hadn't required any seducing. Truth be told, he usually didn't have to make any effort at all.

Shawn took a deep breath and met Rutledge's eyes. "Sir, I..." He swallowed. "Is there any way I can get a better grade? I'll do anything. *Anything*."

Rutledge stared at him.

Then, his eyes narrowed.

"Mr. Wyatt," he said at last. "Are you suggesting what I think you are suggesting?"

Shawn swallowed again. Was he? He wasn't sure himself what he was suggesting. "Um, yeah?"

Rutledge's nostrils flared. He leaned back in his chair and studied him intently. "Please clarify to avoid confusion."

Shawn swept his gaze around the room before looking down at his feet and shrugging. His sneakers were worn, but he couldn't afford new ones. "I think you know, sir."

Silence.

Seconds ticked by.

"I see," Rutledge said. "Lock the door and come over here."

Shawn's stomach lurched. His legs unsteady, he walked to the door and locked it, all the while trying to ignore the panicked little voice in his head that was yelling at him, *What are you doing?*

Looking anywhere but at Rutledge, he rounded the desk and stopped next to his professor, his heart pounding in his throat. Rutledge turned in his chair so that he was facing Shawn now.

Shawn focused his gaze on the dark fabric of the professor's suit.

"On your knees," Rutledge said softly.

Dropping to his knees was almost a relief, as unsteady as his legs were.

Rutledge took his chin with his fingers and tipped his head up, forcing Shawn to meet his gaze.

"I can have you expelled for this," he said.

Shawn's eyes widened.

Rutledge cast him a look of such loathing Shawn flinched. "I have students who never miss classes and work very hard just to get a C. And then there are pretty, empty-headed boys like you who think if they suck my cock, they'll get a good grade."

Shawn felt his face heat up. Hearing the word "cock" from Professor Rutledge was weird as hell.

Weird and downright obscene.

Rutledge's grip on Shawn's chin tightened.

"Do you think it's fair, Wyatt?"

Shawn swallowed, but he forced himself to meet the man's gaze firmly. "If you're going to report this to the board, remember that I didn't say a word about sucking your cock, Professor. You did. If you report me, I'll report you."

A muscle in Rutledge's jaw twitched. "You little shit." His other hand sank into Shawn's hair and yanked him closer to his crotch. "Fine. You want a passing grade? Go ahead. Try to impress me."

Shawn sucked a breath in.

Rutledge smiled. It wasn't a nice smile. "Backing out already?"

"No," Shawn said firmly and reached for the guy's zipper, telling himself it was just a dick. He would suck the guy's dick and get a passing grade. How difficult could it possibly be? It would probably taste disgusting, but it wouldn't kill him or anything.

Right.

Slowly, he unzipped the professor's pants and then… then he stopped. No matter what he told himself, he couldn't move, staring, transfixed, at the bulge under the man's black boxers.

Rutledge let out an irritated noise. "As I thought. Get out, and if you bother me again—"

"No." Shawn shoved a hand into Rutledge's boxers and grabbed his cock.

A beat passed.

Shawn was torn between laughing hysterically and panicking. He had a hand on another guy's cock. *Professor Rutledge's* cock.

It was warm in his hand. That was his first thought. It was growing and becoming thicker with every passing second. It freaked him out a bit, but it also gave him confidence. No matter what Rutledge said, he wanted him.

Shawn gave it an experimental squeeze and looked at the man. Rutledge's face remained impassive. For some reason, that pissed Shawn off. He smiled. "Looks like you have a thing for 'pretty, empty-headed boys,' Professor."

Rutledge's lips pressed together. Otherwise, he looked almost bored. "It's just a physiological reaction to stimuli and a pretty face. You are not responsible for your physical appearance, so it's hardly something to be proud of. Now, if you really intend to do it, stop wasting my time."

Glaring at him, Shawn stroked the cock to full hardness, watching a subtle change in the man's breathing. The angle was awkward, so he pulled the cock out. It was big and thick—and very close to his face. Inches away. Shawn licked his lips nervously, unable to look away. Fucking hell, it had to be at least eight inches long.

Rutledge sighed, as though disgusted with his own body's reaction, and shifted slightly. The head of his cock pressed against Shawn's lips. "Suck."

Shawn inhaled carefully. It didn't smell that bad. Tentatively, he licked the head. The taste was…strange but nowhere near as terrible as he had expected. He licked again.

The professor grunted, his hand gripping Shawn's hair tighter. "Open your mouth." It was an order.

Shawn did as he was told, and the fat head pushed inside his mouth. Shawn sucked gently. A part of his mind was still stuck on the fact that he had Professor Rutledge's dick in his mouth and couldn't quite believe it, but the warmth and heaviness of the cock stretching his lips wide made it very, very real.

Rutledge's eyes were fixed on his face as he pushed his cock deeper, his hand heavy on the back of Shawn's head. Shawn met his gaze, flushed, and closed his eyes, determined to just focus on getting the job done.

The sooner Rutledge came, the sooner it would be over and the sooner he could forget about it.

But with his eyes closed, his other senses came to life and he could feel everything more acutely.

It was…so strange. Rutledge was hard and thick in his mouth, tasting like skin and something else. It was strange, but it wasn't terrible. Shawn pulled off, took a breath and sucked the head in again, going down a bit further, testing it out. He had a brief moment of worry that he wasn't doing this right, but told himself not to be silly: there was no such thing as a bad blowjob, right?

Shawn went down a bit more, trying to take as much of it in as he could. He went down, then back up, setting up a rhythm, trying to get used to it. He was focusing so hard on this, trying to count in his head, that it took him a while before he realized Rutledge was telling him something.

Shawn pulled off the cock with a little pop and looked up at Rutledge, still tasting him all over his tongue. He blinked up at him and had to suppress the ridiculous urge to ask if he was doing okay, like a pupil eager to please his teacher. "What?" he said instead. As usual when he was nervous, his voice came out a bit cocky. He tended to overcompensate sometimes.

Rutledge just looked at him for what seemed like forever, his dark eyes heavy-lidded and glazed over. Eventually he said, "Is this your first dick, Wyatt?" Rutledge's voice was rough and guttural, as though he was the one who'd just spent the past few minutes with a dick in his mouth.

"Does it matter?"

Rutledge's lips twisted. "No. But that explains why you're so bad at it."

Shawn scowled and squeezed the guy's erection. "Your dick seems to think I'm doing all right."

Rutledge sneered. "It just proves how easy we men are." He looked at Shawn's lips. "Go on, but stop overthinking it. You don't think in class, but now you think too hard when you shouldn't be thinking."

Shawn glowered at him but nodded.

He gave Rutledge's dick a few licks before wrapping his lips back around it and doing whatever he wanted, rhythm and concentration be damned.

It was a lot messier this way. He went down as much as he could without choking, came back up and off, licking a long stripe up the underside of Rutledge's dick and tonguing his slit, tasting salty bitterness.

Shawn tried not to think about how obscene he probably looked like this, bobbing his head and dripping spit everywhere as he sucked his teacher's cock. Rutledge was grunting and pushing down on his head, so he was clearly doing something right. Reassured, Shawn kept sucking, working his mouth faster now, ignoring the ache in his jaw and moving his hand faster all along the part of Rutledge's cock he couldn't fit in his mouth.

"Open your eyes," Rutledge bit out.

Shawn did and looked up at him. Their eyes met, and Shawn flushed, acutely aware that his lips were still wrapped tightly around his professor's cock. His professor's cock. Jesus fucking Christ.

"I'm going to fuck your mouth now," Rutledge said, his tone conversational, as though he didn't have his dick in his student's mouth. "Sit back and let me do the job. Look at me."

Shawn felt his cheeks and neck redden, but he did as he was told. Rutledge shifted, his strong, big hands cradling his face. His cock slid out of Shawn's mouth until only the head stayed in it.

Shawn looked at Rutledge.

The man looked back at him and thrust deep into his mouth. Shawn gasped, fighting his gag reflex and trying desperately to breathe around the cock, but he still held his professor's gaze, as instructed.

Rutledge's nostrils flared, his eyes roaming all over Shawn's face. He pulled out and thrust back in. Then again. And again. All the while looking at him. Shawn was sure he was blushing, because it felt incredibly filthy. It was his professor—the most feared professor in school—that was using his mouth to get off. Everything felt too much and overwhelming: the taste, the weight, the feel of Professor Rutledge's cock in his mouth, the strong hands holding his face firmly as Rutledge thrust in and out of his mouth, Rutledge's breath becoming more labored, his dark, intense eyes fixed on Shawn's—

Rutledge bucked his hips and Shawn nearly choked, but he rode it out, feeling hot come hit the back of his throat, spurting in quick succession. Coughing, he let the softening cock out of his mouth.

"Swallow," Rutledge ordered.

Shawn glared up at him but did as he was told, albeit with some difficulty. Thankfully, it didn't taste as gross as he had expected.

Looking down at him through heavy-lidded eyes, Rutledge took a deep breath.

The next moment, his face closed off. He removed his hands and tucked himself in. "Passable."

Shawn didn't know whether to laugh or punch the asshole in the face. He got to his feet, wiped his swollen lips and said, "Thanks, Professor." His voice was hoarse and scratchy—from sucking his professor's cock. "So, what about that grade?"

A muscle pulsed in Rutledge's cheek. He looked downright pissed off. "Dismissed, Wyatt."

Shawn left.

As the door to the professor's office closed behind him, Shawn breathed out. He couldn't believe he'd actually done it. He had sucked another guy's cock. He had let Derek Rutledge, of all people, fuck his mouth in exchange for a grade.

Shawn flushed and looked around, suddenly paranoid that everyone could guess what had happened just from looking at him. But no one was paying him any attention. No one knew.

Everything was fine.

What was done was done. He could put the incident behind him and pretend it had never happened.

Now he could only hope Rutledge would keep his end of the deal.

Chapter Four

"Relax, man," Christian said, dropping into the seat next to him.

"What do you mean?" Shawn said, glancing around the lecture hall before looking at his hands.

"You're tense as hell. Are you nervous about your grades? Didn't you say you talked to Rutledge and convinced him to give you a second chance?"

"Yeah, I did. He didn't fail me yet—I just found out he gave me a D." And god, it had been such a relief. Shawn didn't think he had ever been so happy to receive a D.

"Congrats," Christian said with a grin, patting him on the back. "I'm still amazed you managed to convince him."

Shawn studiously avoided his friend's eyes.

"Speak of the devil," Christian muttered.

The instant hush that fell over the lecture hall was almost amusing. Almost.

Shawn glanced at Rutledge's tall form before dropping his gaze.

"The midterm grades are in," Rutledge said, without preamble. "I reported the grades of thirty-eight students whose grades were below C-. The reports were sent to the Office of the Registrar, which distributed them to the individual students." He paused. "If you have any questions, ask."

Silence.

Some guy lifted his hand.

"Yes, Mr. Taylor?" Rutledge said, walking toward the student. Shawn didn't look; he just saw it in his peripheral vision.

"I don't understand," Taylor said. "I got an F, and apparently that's it! I can't even improve my grade? In every other class, midterm grades don't affect our overall GPA. They're pretty much there to tell us where we are in the class, and whether or not we need to work harder, but apparently, not in your class. What the—I don't get it!"

Shawn cringed.

"Poor guy," Christian muttered.

There was a pause.

"Mr. Taylor," Rutledge said at last, his voice dangerously soft. "Have you read the syllabus?"

"Well, yeah, sure." Taylor sounded anything but sure.

"If you read the syllabus, you would have known that in my class midterm grades do affect your final grades. In other words, if you receive a failing midterm grade, you will not get a passing final grade. No exceptions."

"But it's not fair!" Taylor said. "That's not how

things are done!"

"That's how things are done in my class." If possible, Rutledge's voice became even softer. "I will not pass a student who had an abysmal attendance record for half of the term and failed to turn in his assignments or turned them in late. If you read the syllabus, as I *told* you all to do on the first day of the term, you would not be in this predicament. You can thank only yourself."

Rutledge's lips twisted. "Do you have other questions? Intelligent questions?"

"No," Taylor grumbled.

"Now are we done with that, or does anyone else want to waste my time with pointless questions you're supposed to know the answers to?"

The silence was almost eerie. No one dared to breathe.

"Good." Rutledge returned to his desk.

"Wow," Christian whispered, barely audibly. "What crawled up his ass and died?"

Probably pissed off he couldn't fail me.

His skin prickled. He looked up and found Rutledge giving him a look of such loathing it made him feel like he was being repelled from the room. Shawn lifted his chin and met his gaze firmly. Seriously, what was the guy's problem? It wasn't like he had forced Rutledge to put his dick into his student's mouth.

The thought—the memory—made Shawn blush and shift in his seat uncomfortably. Looking at Rutledge's stony face, it was hard to believe it had really happened.

But it happened.

Shawn glanced at Rutledge's hands—*gripping his face as Rutledge pushed his cock into his mouth—*

Shawn licked his lips, his skin uncomfortably hot, and fixed his gaze in front of him.

He wouldn't think of it.

He wouldn't.

* * *

He had thought he could put the incident out of his mind.

He had thought Rutledge would just ignore him after the incident.

He had been wrong on both counts.

Shawn sighed and stared moodily at the assignment in front of him. Rutledge had been incredibly difficult the past few days, giving him brutally difficult assignments and constantly scolding him in front of everyone when Shawn failed to complete them to Rutledge's satisfaction.

"Are you done, Wyatt?" said a familiar cold voice, and Shawn tensed. He glanced at Christian to his left, but his friend eyed the book in front of him with exaggerated interest. Traitor.

"I'll be done soon," Shawn lied. He stiffened when Rutledge put a hand on the desk and leaned down to look at the blank piece of paper in front of him.

"I see," Rutledge said.

Shawn turned his head to glare at him and was taken aback by how close the other man's face was. Inches away. Dark eyes locked with his for a moment before their owner's lips twisted derisively. Rutledge straightened up to his impressive height and said, "Your assignment is due in ten minutes, Wyatt."

"But you said—"

"Ten minutes," Rutledge repeated.

He walked away, and Shawn glowered at his back.

He returned his gaze to the paper in front of him and stared at it sullenly. It wasn't fair. How was he supposed to complete this assignment in such a short time? The questions were ridiculously difficult and barely reflected what they'd learned in class. Why couldn't the asshole just leave him alone? It felt like Rutledge was determined to make his life a living hell—and he was succeeding.

Shawn scowled, trying to keep his temper in check and failing. He was tired, sleep-deprived, hungry, and angry—never a good combination.

Later, he would blame everything on his sleep-deprivation. He would blame his sleep-deprivation for writing what he would have never written had he not been so damn tired, hungry, and angry.

Shawn turned in his "assignment" exactly ten minutes later and walked back to his desk.

He wasn't even halfway to his desk when Rutledge said, his voice very soft, "Mr. Wyatt, my office after your classes."

His mouth dry, Shawn nodded.

Idiot, he told himself. He shouldn't have let his temper get the better of him.

* * *

When his classes were over, Shawn went to Rutledge's office, as ordered. Taking a deep breath, he knocked on the familiar door.

"Enter."

Shawn went inside and closed the door carefully.

Then he walked to Rutledge's desk.

"Well?" he said, crossing his arms over his chest.

Slowly, Rutledge looked up. The expression on his face was positively stony as he moved a piece of paper towards Shawn—the "assignment" he had turned in. "What is the meaning of this?"

Shawn picked up the paper and reread the single sentence written on it, as though he didn't know what it said.

Do you want to fail me so I have no choice but to suck your dick again?

Inwardly, Shawn was cringing a bit. He couldn't believe he'd lost his temper and actually written that.

But aloud, he said, "Can't you read, sir?" Only a few days ago, he wouldn't have dared to use this cocky tone with Rutledge, but apparently having had the guy's dick in his mouth did wonders.

Rutledge stood up and walked to him.

He came to a halt only a few inches away.

Shawn didn't move, refusing to be intimidated.

"I can have you expelled for this," Rutledge said.

"Sure, but it will get you fired and your career tarnished when everyone finds out you're trading grades for sex."

Rutledge grabbed his neck. "You little shit." His hand tightened on his throat. "Are you threatening me?"

"No," Shawn croaked out. "I just really dislike being bullied. I didn't force you to shove your dick into my mouth, *Professor*."

Rutledge's nostrils flared. He didn't say anything, the muscles in his jaw working.

"Seriously, what's your problem with me?" Shawn said, struggling to breathe through the pressure of Rutledge's grip. "I can't be the only student you used. I'm not proud of what I did, but it was a fair deal: we both got something out of it. Why are you always on my back?"

"I never trade grades for sex," Rutledge ground out. "You were the only exception."

Shawn blinked. "What? But I heard—"

"Yes, I get offers all the time, but I report everyone who's stupid enough to suggest it outright. Do I look like someone who would trade grades for anything, Wyatt?"

Well, no. That was why Shawn had had trouble believing it when Christian had told him the rumor.

"But then…" Shawn studied Rutledge. "Then what about me? Why me?"

The silence stretched.

And stretched. And stretched some more.

Oh.

Shawn licked his lips. "You want me." He let out an uncertain chuckle. "Wow. I'm—I'm kind of flattered, I guess."

Rutledge glowered at him, his grip flexing on Shawn's throat. "It's just lust, nothing more. I won't give you special treatment."

"You're already giving me 'special treatment,' Professor. You've been a total asshole lately—even more than you usually are." Shawn held his gaze. "Let's be honest, man. I needed not to fail your class, so I sucked you off. I didn't force you to accept my offer. You wanted your dick sucked and you got what you wanted. It's not my fault you couldn't resist it. And it sure as hell isn't my fault that I turn you on. So please stop taking it out on me. I get it: you're sexually frustrated, but go jerk off, or fuck someone—"

"I don't think so," Rutledge said, very softly.

Shawn didn't like the gleam in his eyes. "What?"

"I always get what I want," Rutledge said, his soft tone at odds with the hard grip on Shawn's throat. There would probably be bruises. "If I want your mouth, I'll get your mouth, not someone else's. Get on your knees."

Shawn stared at him. Was this guy for real?

"I don't think so, Professor," he said, just as softly. "You're the one who wants his dick sucked. I'm straight. What's in it for me?"

Rutledge's eyes narrowed. "I won't repeat my mistake again. You'll have to work for the final grade like everyone else. I won't give you a grade you don't deserve."

"Then it looks like it will be the first time you don't get what you want. Sir. Let go. Now."

Rutledge didn't let go, his gaze assessing. "Two thousand," he said.

Shawn frowned. "What?"

"Two thousand dollars a month."

Shawn laughed, an incredulous, hard edge to it. "You've got to be kidding me. I'm not a whore."

Rutledge raised his eyebrows.

Shawn scowled, though he felt his cheeks grow hot. "It's different."

"How is that different?" Rutledge's lips curled, but Shawn would never call it a smile. "It's actually far more honest and straightforward than whoring yourself for a grade. You need money, Wyatt."

"How do you know that?" Shawn said sharply.

"I have eyes. Most of your clothes are worn out and old."

Rutledge's tone was matter-of-fact, yet Shawn suddenly felt very conscious of the shabbiness of his appearance compared to Rutledge's immaculate suit. "Don't you have better things to do than study your students' clothes?"

Rutledge stroked his thumb over the pulse in Shawn's neck. "Two thousand a month. Just for sucking my dick. Think about it, Wyatt."

Shawn didn't want to think about it. He wanted to laugh in Rutledge's face and walk out, but…

But.

He thought about the empty fridge and cupboards

at home. He thought about the rent, due next week. He thought about the winter coming soon—and the heating bills. He thought about Mrs. Hawkins's wages. He thought about the fact that he barely saw Emily and Bee, because he had to work two jobs and still barely scraped a living.

He was tempted. Fucking hell, he was tempted. It didn't exactly make him proud, but Rutledge was right: he needed money and he was in no position to be picky about the source of the money.

"Three thousand," Shawn said. If he was going to whore himself out, he wasn't going to be cheap. Rutledge wasn't married, had a cushy job. and had published multiple award-winning books. He could easily afford it.

Rutledge snorted. "You can't be serious. I can find fifty whores for that money."

"I'm sure you can. But it's me you want. And I'm not a whore."

"You could have fooled me."

Shawn ignored the jab and said softly, looking Rutledge in the eye, "It's not like you can't afford it. Three grand for fucking my mouth any time you want."

Rutledge's nostrils flared. His face was hard to read, but the hunger in his eyes as he looked at Shawn's lips was harder to conceal. It made Shawn feel weird. He was straight, but he was honest enough with himself to admit that it *was* flattering as hell that this man—this powerful man everyone feared and respected—wanted him so badly.

"Any time I want?" Rutledge said, lifting his gaze

to Shawn's eyes.

After a moment's hesitation, Shawn nodded.

How often could Rutledge possibly demand for him to do it? Probably a few times a week, at most. About ten times a month. And he'd get three thousand dollars for that. He would be able to quit one of his jobs and spend more time with the kids.

It would be worth it.

"Very well," Rutledge said, letting go of his throat. He returned to his chair and looked at Shawn. "What are you waiting for, Wyatt?"

Shawn swallowed and looked down at the impressive bulge in the man's pants. He could totally do it. Just ten times a month and three thousand dollars for his trouble. He had already sucked Rutledge's dick once and it wasn't revolting or anything. He could do it.

Shawn locked the door and then sank to his knees in front of the most hated professor in school.

Chapter Five

I really underestimated his sex drive, Shawn thought as he sucked his professor's cock a week later. It was the fifth time that week that he'd found himself on his knees in front of Rutledge.

Shawn had to admit it wasn't disgusting or anything; it could have been worse. Much worse. Rutledge's dick was always clean and tasted all right. Sure, the size made it more difficult than it could have been, but after the first few times, he'd gotten used to it and his jaw had stopped aching. Besides, more often than not, Rutledge did most of the job, holding Shawn's face in place and just fucking into his mouth.

However, there were times, like today, when Rutledge ordered Shawn to lick and suck his cock slowly. That was more difficult, but Shawn's inner sense of fairness didn't let him do a half-assed job: Rutledge paid him a lot of money for this, after all.

If anyone had told him a few weeks ago that he would be sucking another guy's dick every day, Shawn would have laughed. If anyone had told him that he would let Professor Rutledge, of all people, put his dick in his mouth every day, Shawn would have thought it was a very bad joke.

And not a funny joke.

Yet there he was, sucking Rutledge's cock, Rutledge's big hand guiding his head as Shawn bobbed his head, swirling his tongue around the head of his teacher's cock. Yeah, it did taste all right. Shawn found that with each time he minded the taste less.

Rutledge grunted, his hips bucking up slightly. Shawn wasn't sure what it said about him that he could tell Rutledge was close.

"Look at me," Rutledge demanded.

Shawn met the dark eyes and sucked on the head slowly. Then harder.

Rutledge grabbed Shawn's hair, thrust hard, and came.

Shawn swallowed the come. He wasn't a fan of the taste, but he knew Rutledge liked when he did it. The taste wasn't that horrible, anyway.

After a while, he felt Rutledge's gaze on him and he looked up again.

Rutledge was staring at him with an odd expression on his face. Suddenly, Shawn realized that he still had Rutledge's soft cock in his mouth and was still sucking on it idly, as though it was a giant lollipop.

Flushing, Shawn let the cock slip out of his mouth and shot to his feet. "I just zoned out," he said, turning away and wiping his mouth.

"I didn't say anything," Rutledge said.

When he heard the sound of a zipper, Shawn

turned back.

Once again, Professor Rutledge looked immaculate and untouchable. If Shawn didn't know better, he would never believe what had just transpired in this office a few minutes ago.

Shawn shifted from one foot to the other.

Leaning back in his chair, Rutledge raised his eyebrows. "Yes?"

Shit. This was awkward as hell, but Mrs. Hawkins had told him that she would quit if Shawn didn't raise her wages. To make matters worse, his rent was due today. So Shawn forced himself to speak, "I need money. Can you pay me now? I mean—I know it wasn't the deal, but—"

"Come over here."

Shawn closed his mouth mid-sentence and stepped toward him. He couldn't read Rutledge's expression.

Rutledge took his wrist and yanked him into his lap.

"What the—"

"What's in it for me?" Rutledge said, clearly mocking him by using the words Shawn had said a week ago.

Shawn gripped the back of Rutledge's chair, feeling uncomfortable and weirded out. He'd never imagined he would ever be in this situation: sitting in Professor Rutledge's lap and trying to cajole money out of him. "What do you want? Another blowjob?"

Rutledge studied him.

"You let me kiss you and touch you, and I will give you the money."

Shawn blinked. He looked down at Rutledge's lips and felt an uneasy feeling spread in his stomach. "I don't know—I mean, I'm straight. That would be kind of weird."

The lips he was looking at twisted.

"More weird than sucking my cock, Wyatt?"

Shawn felt nervous laughter bubble up inside him. "Well, when you put it that way, I guess you're right."

Rutledge wrapped a hand around Shawn's neck, stroking his pulse with his thumb. "Well?"

Shawn shrugged. "Fine. Whatever."

It seemed as though Rutledge had been waiting for just those words, because the next thing Shawn knew, he had his professor's tongue in his mouth. Shawn's eyes widened, but he forced himself to relax.

He closed his eyes, trying to distance himself from what was happening and failing. Surprisingly, Rutledge was a pretty good kisser. He wasn't sloppy, and the kiss wasn't gross, but it was *strange.* It was strange to be the one being kissed, not the other way around. He was being kissed by a man, not a girl. The difference shouldn't have been so obvious, but it was. Rutledge kissed the same way he acted: bossy, demanding, and hard.

A few minutes later, when Rutledge was finally done kissing him, Shawn's lips were swollen and sensitive. He felt kind of overwhelmed and more than a little weirded out.

Rutledge took one look at him, snorted, and pushed him off his lap. Shawn got to his feet unsteadily and turned to leave.

"You didn't collect your payment, Wyatt."

Payment. Right.

Shawn turned back and didn't look at him as Rutledge put money into his pocket.

"Now get out," Rutledge said. "I have papers to grade."

Shawn was only all too happy to obey.

Once he was outside the office, he touched his sore lips.

They were tingling.

Chapter Six

Turned out, kissing wasn't just a one-time thing. Rutledge seemed to think that now that he'd done it once, he had the right to shove his tongue into Shawn's mouth whenever he wanted—and he seemed to want it very often.

As a result, Shawn had been spending an awful lot of time in Rutledge's lap, with Rutledge's tongue in his mouth and Rutledge's hands on his ass. The latter made him a bit uneasy, but Rutledge didn't seem to want anything else. Shawn figured the guy just couldn't help it, so he didn't make a fuss about it.

Usually, after about ten minutes of hard kissing, Rutledge ordered him to suck him off, but today he was taking his time, kissing him over and over, deep and absolutely filthy, until Shawn could barely breathe. The familiar feeling of being completely overwhelmed was back, and Shawn found himself gasping and making small noises—he wasn't even sure why. It was just too much. He wasn't sure whether he liked this feeling—the feeling of being completely overwhelmed—or hated it.

At last, Rutledge broke the kiss, but instead of simply ordering him to suck him off, as he usually did, he started kissing Shawn's neck.

"Er, I'm pretty sure this wasn't part of the deal," Shawn said.

Rutledge ignored him, of course.

Shawn rolled his eyes. Since the whole thing started, he'd discovered that Rutledge actually kept himself in check in class and did not demonstrate the extent of his…personality. When they were alone, Rutledge didn't hold back: he was completely domineering. Everything had to be done the way Rutledge wanted.

Shawn was torn away from his thoughts when he felt Rutledge's large hands slide under his shirt to stroke his bare back.

"You're kinda crossing the line, man," Shawn murmured, though if he was honest with himself, he wasn't that bothered by Rutledge's coping a feel. He wondered whether he should be.

It wasn't the first time it had occurred to Shawn that he was nowhere near as freaked out by the whole thing as he probably should have been. But then again, he had the guy's dick in his mouth every day. This was nothing.

Rutledge continued to nibble at his neck aggressively. "Pull me out and jerk me off."

Before Shawn could do it, Rutledge's cell phone started vibrating on the desk.

Swearing through his teeth, Rutledge lifted his head from Shawn's neck and reached out for his phone.

"Yes?" he snapped without looking at the caller ID.

Shawn watched with interest as Rutledge's face turned into a stony mask. He obviously didn't like whatever the caller was saying to him, because his voice turned hard. "I'm not interested, Vivian." A pause. "I don't give a damn about what he wants. Save your breath. I'm not coming."

His curiosity piqued, Shawn leaned closer to the phone, trying to catch what she was saying.

"…father is very ill, Derek," the woman—Vivian—said. "I swear I'm not lying. He would never admit it, but I know he wants to see you before—before… Please. For me."

Rutledge's jaw tightened. "I'm not going to do what he wants me to do. I'm not marrying that silly little girl."

"Amanda is a nice young woman," Vivian said. "Yes, her dad is our father's friend, but she's not her dad. She's kind and—"

"Vivian," Rutledge cut her off, glaring at his desk. "You're forgetting something. I'm not into women. And even if I were, I would have never married the woman he chose for me."

Vivian sighed. "Just come home this weekend. That's the only thing I'm asking."

Rutledge pinched the bridge of his nose. "Fine," he bit out. He hung up rudely and dropped the phone onto his desk.

"Your sister?" Shawn said. Figuring Rutledge wasn't in the mood for sex anymore, he was about to slide off his lap when Rutledge grabbed him and yanked him into a kiss.

The kiss was cruel, hard, and punishing. It ended as quickly as it started. Rutledge gripped his chin and stared at him, anger still rolling off him in waves. "You will accompany me."

Shawn chuckled. "I will? Thanks for informing me."

"I'll pay you," Rutledge said, not at all fazed. "Another three thousand for the weekend."

Shawn stared at him. "You can't be serious. You're willing to pay me three grand just to annoy your dad?"

The glare Rutledge gave him would have made him flinch a few weeks ago. "That's none of your business." He glanced at his watch. "It's almost two. Go home and pack for the weekend. I'll pick you up in two hours."

Shawn put his hands on Rutledge's shoulders. "Whoa, wait a second. I'm not going anywhere. I'm serious. I can't."

Rutledge shot him an irritated look. "Why not?"

Shawn hesitated. "I have two little sisters. They're just four. I can't leave them for the weekend. They have no one else."

Rutledge had an expression on his face Shawn couldn't quite read. "Get them a babysitter. I'll pay."

Rolling his eyes, Shawn jumped off his lap. "Is that your answer to everything? You can't buy everything, you know. I'm not going to leave the kids with someone they don't know. Their usual babysitter has a weekend off."

Rutledge heaved a sigh, his brows knitting slightly as a frown crossed his lips.

"Fine. Bring the brats with us."

Shawn paused before turning back to him. "I don't think it's a good idea. They get anxious around strangers, and you…well, you're you."

A wry smile appeared on Rutledge's face. "Contrary to popular opinion, I don't eat babies for breakfast." He stood up and walked toward Shawn. "You're coming with me," he said, stopping in front of him. "I don't care what you do about the children, but you will come with me."

Before Shawn could say anything, Rutledge grabbed his collar and pulled him into a kiss.

A few minutes later Rutledge finally let him breathe again, and Shawn was disturbed to find his fingers clenched in Rutledge's shirt.

"Right," he said, somewhat dazedly, blinking.

Rutledge gave him a push towards the door. "I'll pick you up in two hours. I know your address."

"Right," Shawn said again and left, feeling more than a little confused and freaked out.

Chapter Seven

"But where are we going?" Emily asked, pulling at Shawn's hand.

"Who's gonna come and pick us up?" Bee asked, bouncing excitedly and pulling at his other hand.

Shawn looked between their excited little faces and grimaced inwardly. This was a terrible idea.

"A friend," he said, choosing to answer Bee, since he had no idea where they were going. Presumably to visit Rutledge's father. It seemed Rutledge and his father were at odds—to put it mildly—so Shawn doubted it was going to be a warm family reunion, even without taking into account the fact that Rutledge was clearly bringing him along just to annoy his father.

Dragging Emily and Bee into this wasn't a good idea, but on the other hand…three thousand dollars. He wouldn't have to worry about Mrs. Hawkins's wages for a few months.

"Is that him? Is that him?" Bee's bouncing became even more excited as she pointed at the black Mercedes that had stopped in front of the building.

"Probably," Shawn said. "Let's go." He took their suitcase and grabbed Bee's hand with his other hand. Emily could be trusted to stay close and not to run off somewhere.

The Mercedes's doors opened when they reached it.

Shawn was surprised to find that Rutledge already had child safety seats installed.

"Hey," he said to Rutledge, feeling awkward and thrown off-balance. Rutledge was never supposed to meet his sisters. "Emily, Melissa, say hello to Mr. Rutledge."

"I'm not Melissa!" Bee said with a pout.

Shawn hid a smile. "Emily, Bee, say hello to Mr. Rutledge."

"Hello, Mr. Rutledge!" they said together and Shawn felt a surge of pride. They were just four, but they were very smart and articulate. They looked like little golden-haired angels, smiling shyly at the man. Anyone with a heart would have smiled back.

Apparently, not Derek Rutledge. Rutledge studied the girls as if they were some strange creatures from another planet before nodding faintly and turning back to Shawn. "Get them into their seats. I'll put your suitcase into the trunk."

Shawn just rolled his eyes, wondering what had turned Rutledge into such a control freak. It was a completely unnecessary order.

By the time the girls were secured in the back, Rutledge had returned to the driver's seat. Shawn glanced at the girls for the last time before closing the door carefully and taking his seat.

"Before we leave, I want to make something clear," Shawn said, lowering his voice so that the girls couldn't hear. "I know very little about your family, but you won't drag the girls into your problems with your father. If anyone treats them badly, we'll leave. Screw the money. Got it?"

Rutledge stared at him for a moment.

"No one will treat them badly," he said before leaning over, grabbing Shawn's chin and covering Shawn's lips with his.

Shawn frowned—it was neither the time nor the place—but Rutledge held his face firmly, his lips hard and hungry, his tongue delving deep into Shawn's mouth, confident and proprietary, and soon enough, Shawn found himself completely overwhelmed by the intensity of the kiss. It went on, and on, and on—

"Shawn, are you hurt?"

With a gasp, he shoved Rutledge away and focused his gaze on Emily. "What? No!"

A furrow appeared between her small brows. "I thought you were hurt. You were making noises."

His face warm, Shawn determinedly avoided looking at Rutledge. "I wasn't making noises."

"You were!" Bee said, looking puzzled. "Lying is bad! You said so!"

Emily nodded. "And why did Mr. Rutledge put his tongue in your mouth?"

"Because your brother wanted something to suck on," Rutledge commented, starting the engine.

Flushing, Shawn kicked him on the shin, but to his surprise, the twins seemed satisfied with the explanation and started talking about something else.

He settled back into his seat.

Shawn didn't look at Rutledge. He couldn't.

He was still warm all over, his skin tight and his breathing uneven.

Fuck. What was happening to him?

* * *

"So, what's the deal with your dad?"

They had been driving for over an hour and the girls were asleep.

Rutledge's eyes were fixed on the road ahead. "Since when is it your business?"

"I don't know," Shawn said, not without sarcasm. "You're dragging me—and my family—to your father's house, uninvited. Something tells me he won't be happy to see us."

"He won't. But if it makes you feel better, he won't be happy to see me, either."

Shawn leaned back in his seat and studied his profile. "I thought he invited you."

Rutledge chuckled. It was a chilling sound. "My father would never swallow his pride and invite me. Fifteen years ago, he said I would come crawling back when I ran out of money. He hates being wrong."

Shawn's eyes widened. "You mean you haven't been home in fifteen years?"

"And I'd gladly stay away for fifteen more years. I'm still not convinced my sister isn't lying about his health. That old bastard will outlive us all."

Shawn was a little disturbed. What did Rutledge's father do to deserve such hatred from his own son?

"Um, did he beat you when you were a kid?"

The corner of Rutledge's mouth twitched. "Joseph Rutledge would never do something so plebeian."

"Ah." Shawn hesitated. "Did he kick you out because of your sexuality?"

Rutledge's fingers gripped the steering wheel tighter. "He never kicked me out. I left myself."

Shawn could sense it was more complicated than that. If Rutledge's father wanted his son to marry some woman, it meant he still hadn't accepted his son's sexuality; he probably thought it was something "curable." But since Shawn didn't know Rutledge's father, he could only speculate.

"What's he like?"

Rutledge shrugged slightly. "Typical old money. Proud, high-handed, and inflexible."

"Hmm, he reminds me of someone, then."

Rutledge visibly stiffened.

Shawn took in the tense set of his wide shoulders, the aggressive jut of his profile. The five o'clock shadow gave him a rugged, rougher look. Shawn's eyes trailed down Rutledge's arms, from his biceps straining beneath the sleeves of his shirt to the fingers gripping the steering wheel a little tighter than necessary.

Shawn licked his dry lips, staring at Rutledge's hands. He remembered them gripping his chin, his neck—

"You keep looking at me that way and you'll end up with my dick in you before the trip is over."

Shawn snapped his gaze to Rutledge's face. Rutledge was looking at the road ahead.

His face hot, Shawn said, "I don't know what you're talking about."

Rutledge just snorted.

Silence fell between them, thick, charged, tingling with awareness.

Finally, Shawn couldn't stand it anymore. "What did you mean?"

"You know what I mean. Despite your poor grades, you are not completely stupid."

"Wow, thanks. I'm going to mark this day in the calendar. 'Professor Rutledge said I'm not completely stupid.' I feel so special, you know."

"Wyatt." Rutledge still wouldn't look at Shawn. "You're not as straight as you believe. To put it bluntly: you look at me like you want to suck my cock."

Shawn opened his mouth but closed it without saying anything. Then he laughed. "You have a really high opinion of yourself."

Rutledge sighed, pulled the car off the road and killed the engine. Without a word, he got out of the car, walked to the passenger seat, opened the door and dragged Shawn out.

"Hey!" Shawn said, glancing back at the twins, but they were still sound asleep.

Rutledge shut the door and dragged Shawn away from the car, towards the woods.

"Look—" Shawn started, but he was cut off when Rutledge pushed him against the wide trunk of a tree and put his hands by either side of Shawn's face.

The dark eyes bored into him. "I have no patience for gay freak outs. I couldn't care less if you delude yourself into thinking that you're totally straight. But when you're with me, I don't want to hear this nonsense."

Shawn laughed uncertainly. "Don't you think it's a bit presumptuous of you to say you know better than me whether I'm straight or gay?"

"Actually, I think you're bisexual, but it's neither here nor there. I'm not saying I know better than you what turns you on. But I have eyes. I can easily tell when a guy wants to suck my dick."

"I don't want to suck your dick. I suck your dick only because you pay me to do it."

"Yes, I pay you," Rutledge said in a low voice. "But it doesn't mean you don't like it. You have a bit of an oral fixation, Wyatt. Your mouth is very sensitive. You like having your mouth full. You like being kissed. You like being fucked in the mouth."

Shawn shivered. "I don't."

Rutledge raised his eyebrows. "You continue sucking my dick even after I come."

His skin growing warm, Shawn averted his gaze. Yeah, he had caught himself doing that a few times, but… "Even if what you say is true, it doesn't prove anything." Oral fixation was actually a good explanation why he enjoyed Rutledge's kisses and why having Rutledge's dick in his mouth felt kind of…all right.

"You're right," Rutledge said. "Liking to suck another man's dick doesn't make you gay."

"Stop mocking me."

"I'm not mocking you."

They looked at each other in silence.

Shawn moistened his lips with a swipe of his tongue.

Rutledge lifted his hand and stroked Shawn's bottom lip with his thumb.

Shawn stayed very still, barely breathing.

Rutledge slowly pushed the thumb into his mouth, gently parting Shawn's lips, as they continued to stare at each other. Shawn tentatively brushed the tip of his tongue over the thumb and then...

He sucked.

Rutledge inhaled sharply. He began to push and pull his thumb in and out of Shawn's mouth, all the while looking him in the eye.

It made Shawn blush—he was sucking on his professor's thumb, for fuck's sake—but god help him, he was loving it, the inside of his mouth tingling. He couldn't stop sucking. He wanted to keep sucking on it.

He made a small noise when Rutledge removed his thumb.

"Definitely oral fixation," Rutledge murmured before leaning in and replacing his thumb with his tongue.

Several minutes later, Shawn found himself on the grass, with Rutledge's heavy body on top of him. He was moaning as he sucked greedily on Rutledge's tongue, his hands buried in the man's hair. He couldn't pretend anymore that he didn't enjoy this, so he didn't try to suppress his sighs and moans of pleasure as Rutledge thoroughly fucked his mouth with his tongue.

"You're noisy," Rutledge grunted, nipping along Shawn's jawline and down his neck.

Shawn felt too disoriented to answer and only pulled him back to his lips. He wanted more kisses. He needed more kisses. Rutledge obliged, kissing him deeply, his hand fumbling between them, doing…something.

Shawn's eyes widened when he felt Rutledge wrap his hand around both of their cocks. He tensed. He was hard. He was *hard*.

"Forget about labels, goddammit," Rutledge said and started stroking them fast, kissing Shawn deeper and dirtier.

Shawn could do nothing but moan. He was too far gone to protest. He wanted to come. Before he could stop himself, he started moving his hips, meeting Rutledge's strokes, feeling Rutledge's cock rub against his, and fuck, the mere thought—it was wrong and arousing all at once.

It didn't take long. They weren't even kissing now—more like trying to swallow each other, lips and teeth biting and sucking. Shawn rolled a little and hooked one leg up over Rutledge's, bracing them together. Fire burned through him in a white-hot glow, and he could feel it gathering in his belly, spreading outward in streaks.

He felt Rutledge growl, low and rough, shuddering as he came, sticky wet heat pooling between them. A few more strokes and Shawn was coming too, moaning and clawing at Rutledge's back.

He opened his eyes slowly and found Rutledge already on his feet, zipping his pants up.

Realizing his cock was still out in the open, Shawn quickly tucked himself in and zipped up, his fingers shaking.

He could hear Rutledge walk back to the car. "One of them is awake."

Shawn got to his feet. "Them?" he said, still unable to think about anything besides the fact that he'd just had sex with a man.

"One of the children," Rutledge said, getting into the driver's seat. The way Rutledge said the word "children," he could as well be talking about aliens. It almost made Shawn smile. Almost.

Shawn walked to the car and took his seat.

Bee was still asleep, but Emily wasn't. She was sucking on her thumb sleepily, looking between Shawn and Rutledge. "You weren't here when I woke up."

Shawn leaned over and kissed her on the forehead. "I'm sorry, baby. Were you scared?"

"I'm not a baby," Emily said. "I'm big. We're there already?"

"No," Shawn said.

"Then why did the car stop?"

Shawn cleared his throat. How was he supposed to answer that? "Because Mr. Rutledge and I needed to talk."

Rutledge started the engine.

Emily yawned. "Why couldn't you talk in the car?"

"Because—because we didn't want to wake you up."

Emily frowned but seemed to accept the explanation. Her eyes started closing again.

Breathing out, Shawn turned away from her and looked at the passing scenery.

"Put on the seatbelt," Rutledge ordered after a while.

Shawn put on the seatbelt and muttered, "Control freak."

"So are you done freaking out?" Rutledge's tone was sardonic.

"I wasn't freaking out." Realizing he said it a bit too loud, Shawn lowered his voice. "Why would I? So you gave me a hand-job. Big deal. I haven't had sex in ages, and you know kissing turns me on."

Rutledge said nothing and returned his gaze to the road, his face completely unreadable.

Shawn studied him. "You know, I'm curious about something," he murmured. "Why me? Why do you pay me an obscene amount of money for a few blowjobs? You don't even need to pay for sex. I'm sure lots of gay men would gladly have sex with you. I mean, it's not like you're ugly or something. So why me?"

"Are you fishing for compliments?"

"Nope. I'm genuinely curious."

"I wanted to fuck you since the moment you entered my classroom a few months ago. It's as simple as that."

Shawn moistened his lips, his stomach doing a little flip-flop. "You wanted me for that long?"

Rutledge snorted, without looking at him.

"I wasn't pining or anything, Wyatt. I wanted to get my dick in you. You're just my type."

"Blond?"

"No. I don't mean your looks. If we go by looks alone, your friend, Ashford, is more my type than you."

Shawn's gut clenched. He wasn't sure why he was surprised. Christian was extremely attractive. Hell, everyone was attracted to him. And with his dark brown hair, expressive brown eyes and sensual red lips, he was Shawn's complete opposite. Shawn always felt pale and washed out next to his friend.

"So if it was Christian who offered sex for a grade, you'd do it?"

Rutledge shot him a strange look. "No."

The muscles in Shawn's gut unclenched. "Why not?"

"Because I don't want to fuck him," Rutledge said crudely. He was starting to look irritated, for some reason. "Finding someone physically attractive isn't the same thing as wanting them."

"So what did you mean when you said I'm your type?"

Rutledge was quiet for so long Shawn started to think he wasn't going to reply at all.

There was a touch of self-deprecation in his voice when he spoke, "It's all very cliché. When I was in school, I was a stereotypical unpopular nerd."

"Really?" Looking at this self-assured, arrogant man, Shawn had trouble believing that.

"Of course I was. I got my PhD at twenty-three, Wyatt. I didn't exactly have the time to socialize with people."

"That explains a lot," Shawn muttered. "Let me guess: there was a popular jock you had a crush on and I look like him?"

"He looked nothing like you."

"Then how is that relevant?"

"If you stop interrupting me, you'll find out." Rutledge's lips curled. "He was the stereotypical popular jock. Obviously straight as an arrow and acted like he owned the world, and I wanted… I looked at him and imagined forcing my dick down his throat. Imagined holding him down and making him beg to be fucked. Making a straight boy beg for my cock."

Shawn swallowed and glanced at the girls to make sure they were asleep. "Where are you going with this?"

Rutledge shrugged slightly, his eyes on the road. "Pretty, straight, and unattainable: that's pretty much my type. If you let me fuck you, I'll get bored of you. I always get bored of them."

Shawn crossed his arms over his chest, feeling cold all of a sudden. "Who's done it to you?" he asked at last, looking at the passing countryside. It was getting dark.

"What?"

"Someone fucked you up." Shawn turned his head to him. "It's not healthy to enter into relationships knowing they're doomed to fail—that you would lose interest in the guy after you fuck him. And it's really fucked up to have straight, unattainable guys as your type. Are you afraid of commitment? Or of something else?"

Rutledge's jaw was clenched so tightly that the cords on his neck stood out. "Spare me your pseudo-psychological analysis. The explanation is actually much simpler: I just like corrupting and fucking straight boys. It turns me on. And before you call me an asshole: I'm always honest with them. Most bi-curious 'straight' guys eventually want to go back to their straight lives anyway, and I don't do long-term relationships. So it's a win-win for everyone involved. No strings attached."

"Why don't you do long-term relationships? You're thirty-three."

"And?" Rutledge said. "I'm not the kind of man who wants the white picket fence and 2.5 kids."

Shawn glanced at Emily and Bee. "I don't know," he said slowly. "I always thought gay guys weren't much different from straight guys and would want to settle down eventually. Even Christian wants that."

"Christian?" Rutledge looked slightly puzzled.

Shawn frowned. "My best friend?"

"Ah. You mean Ashford."

"Seriously? You don't know his name?"

"Why would I want to know his first name? He's my student."

"I'm your student, too, Professor."

Rutledge looked at him, the corner of his mouth twitching up. "Who says I know your first name, Wyatt?"

Shawn laughed softly.

"Okay. For your information, it's Simon."

"No, it isn't."

"A-ha!"

Shaking his head, Rutledge looked back at the road. "I obviously know your name, but I don't think of you as Shawn."

"Fair enough. I don't think of you as Derek, either." Even saying the name aloud was a bit strange, actually. Shawn rolled the name on his tongue. Derek. Nope. Rutledge was Rutledge. Shawn would be very worried the day he started thinking of Rutledge as Derek.

"I'm glad we understand each other," Rutledge murmured, a hint of amusement in his voice. "Now come here and kiss me."

Shawn blinked. "What? You're driving. It's not safe."

"I'll keep my eyes open," Rutledge said dryly, without looking at him.

Shawn looked at the road—it was empty in both directions, and Rutledge was driving slowly, but still.

"Are you serious?"

"You should know by now I'm always serious. I'm losing my patience."

He should say no. It was insane.

Shawn looked at Rutledge's lips and said, "Okay. But just a short one. It's not safe."

He scooted over.

Rutledge turned his head slightly and kissed him. Shawn sighed and let Rutledge's tongue inside.

After… some time later, Rutledge bit Shawn's bottom lip for the last time and pushed him away.

"You should let me fuck you," he said grimly.

Leaning back in his seat, Shawn wiped his wet, swollen lips and took a deep breath. His skin still burned from Rutledge's stubble.

Chapter Eight

It was dark by the time they arrived.

As they got out of the car, Shawn looked up at the house and said, not without humor, "Actually, now some things about you are starting to make a horrible amount of sense."

It was almost laughable to call it a house.

Bee clapped her hands in excitement. "A palace!"

"Don't be stupid," Emily said, her tone superior. "Kings and princesses live in palaces. Our country doesn't have loyalty."

"Royalty," Rutledge corrected her, locking the car. "If you're going to call someone stupid, make sure you don't make mistakes yourself."

Bee beamed at Rutledge and grabbed his hand. "I like you, Mr. Rutledge!"

Rutledge stared down at the tiny girl with a vaguely puzzled expression on his face, before looking at Shawn.

Suppressing a smile, Shawn said, "Leave Mr. Rutledge alone, Bee. Come on, take my hand."

Bee pouted but let go of Rutledge's hand and took Shawn's. Emily took his other hand while a few servants came out to take their luggage inside.

"I don't like him," Emily said as they walked to the house.

"Don't be rude, sweetie," Shawn said, glancing at the man in question, who walked alongside them. "Mr. Rutledge can hear you."

Rutledge's eyes were focused on the house; he showed no sign of listening to the conversation.

Shawn averted his gaze. It was hard to believe that just a few hours ago, he had this immaculately dressed, stern-faced man grunting and moving on top of him.

"But I don't like him," Emily said stubbornly but lowered her voice. "Don't like how he looks at you."

"How he looks at me?" Shawn repeated.

"Like Bee looks at a pancake."

Shawn forced a smile. This was a whole new level of awkward. "You just imagined it, pumpkin."

"But—"

"You just imagined it," Shawn repeated, hoping Rutledge hadn't heard Emily's words.

Rutledge's face was hard and cold, devoid of all color. This was a man who was coming home to his father after fifteen years. He looked about as happy as a man on his way to jail.

A butler—a goddamn butler—opened the door and greeted Rutledge with a quiet,

"Master Derek."

Shawn led the girls inside. They looked shy and nervous, and Shawn had to admit he wasn't any less nervous than them; he was simply better at disguising it.

His first impression of the hall was of vastness. It was more than a little overwhelming.

"Derek!"

Shawn looked up. A tall, dark-haired woman was walking down the stairs, a vaguely relieved smile on her lips.

She hugged Rutledge and kissed him on the cheek.

"Vivian," Rutledge murmured. "You look good."

So this was the sister who had convinced him to come.

Shawn eyed her curiously. He could certainly see the family resemblance. She seemed a few years older than her brother, perhaps thirty-five.

Vivian pulled back and stared at Shawn and the girls over Rutledge's shoulder, but before she or Shawn could say anything, two elderly men entered the house.

One of them, the taller one, bore an uncanny resemblance to Rutledge. In fact, they could have been twins if the man wasn't about thirty years older. Shawn decided this must be Rutledge's father, Joseph Rutledge.

"The prodigal son returns," Joseph said with a sneer. "I knew this day would come."

"Then you were wrong," Rutledge said coldly. "I came only because Vivian wouldn't stop nagging me. Apparently, you're practically on your deathbed."

"Derek!" Vivian said, looking outraged.

"I'll have to disappoint you, then," Joseph said. "I'm in excellent health." He was lying. He had an almost gray tinge to his complexion. "So you won't get my money any time soon."

"You know I don't need your money," Rutledge said.

They glared at each other icily, and the resemblance they shared was striking. Shawn wondered if Rutledge knew it and resented it.

At this moment, Joseph shifted his gaze to Shawn.

His sharp dark eyes swept over him from head to toe, making Shawn painfully aware of his worn, cheap clothes.

Rutledge senior's lips twisted in derision. "And this?"

Rutledge took a step toward Shawn and put a hand on his shoulder. "This is my lover, Shawn Wyatt."

The other old man inhaled sharply.

Joseph's face betrayed nothing, yet somehow, the temperature in the room seemed to drop a dozen degrees.

Shawn grimaced on the inside, but it wasn't as if he hadn't expected that.

"Shawn, this is my father, Joseph Rutledge," Rutledge said, his voice uncharacteristically soft. The asshole was absolutely enjoying this. "And my father's old friend, Nathan Brooks."

"Nice to meet you," Shawn lied, wondering if Mr. Brooks was the man whose daughter Joseph wanted his son to marry.

"I see," Joseph said at last before shifting his heavy gaze to the twins. "And these are?"

Shawn suppressed the urge to hide the girls behind his back. "These are my sisters, Mr. Rutledge. Emily and Melissa." For once, Bee remained quiet and didn't argue about her name. Both girls moved closer to Shawn.

"I see," Joseph Rutledge said again before addressing a maid. "Prepare rooms for our guests."

"Prepare a room next to mine for the children," Rutledge cut in. "Obviously Shawn will stay in mine."

Shawn cringed a bit.

The vein in Joseph's temple throbbed. Vivian watched her father worriedly. Mr. Brooks had a look of disgust on his face that he didn't even bother to hide.

"Do as he says," Joseph Rutledge bit out, breaking the silence. "Show them to their rooms. Dinner is in half an hour. Derek, a word."

Shawn turned to follow the maid when a hand grabbed his arm and stopped him.

"I'll see you shortly," Rutledge said and gave him a brief kiss.

Or at least it was probably supposed to be a brief kiss, but
Shawn found his lips clinging and parting, eager. He felt Rutledge's surprise before Rutledge grabbed his neck and kissed him for real.

The kiss seemed to go on forever.

By the time Rutledge finally pulled back, Shawn could barely breathe.

Shawn didn't look around to see everyone's reaction—he could well imagine it.

Grabbing the girls, he followed the maid.

His face was very warm.

Chapter Nine

To say the dinner was awkward would be an understatement. It wasn't just awkward: it was painful.

It was only ten minutes in and Shawn was already glancing at the clock on the wall.

The toxic atmosphere in the room was so thick it could be sliced. He'd never seen so much passive-aggressiveness between family members. Now Shawn was glad Emily and Bee hadn't been allowed to eat with the adults.

The annoying part was, no one said anything outright; everything was carefully hidden behind bland smiles and polished manners. Andrew, Vivian's husband, was the only one who seemed to be struggling to hide his dislike for his brother-in-law.

Rutledge didn't pay Andrew much mind, though; his most cutting remarks were reserved for his father. Rutledge was rather infamous for his ruthlessness in college, but it was nothing compared to his nastiness towards his father.

Shawn would have felt sorry for Joseph Rutledge if the old man wasn't actually worse. Within the first ten minutes, Joseph had managed to insult everything from his son's intelligence to his sexuality, his tone full of derision and contempt.

Watching them, Shawn was beginning to understand why Rutledge had left his home and hadn't returned in fifteen years.

He was also beginning to understand why Rutledge was such a control freak. His father's personality was so domineering that he had likely developed the similar need to control everything as a defense mechanism.

"They do realize how much they're alike, right?" Shawn murmured to Vivian, making sure that Rutledge, who sat on his other side, couldn't hear him. Vivian seemed to be the only friendly face at the table.

She sighed. "I think that's partly why they hate each other," she murmured. "Though deep down, they care for one another."

Shawn looked at the father and son sniping at each other and gave her a skeptical look.

Vivian smiled humorlessly. "I know, it's hard to believe, but Father does care about Derek." Her eyes became distant. "When we were kids, Father used to be very proud of him. I used to envy Derek. Things became…difficult when Father found out about Derek's sexuality, but I'm sure he still cares. If he didn't, he would have disowned him ages ago and removed him from his will."

Glancing at her husband, she lowered her voice.

"Andrew is really angry about it. He's been working at the family company for years and thinks he deserves to inherit it."

"Ah," Shawn said. That explained Andrew's animosity.

Speaking of the man, Andrew chose that moment to turn to Shawn and ask, "So, do you work? Or does my brother-in-law pay your bills for spreading your legs for him?"

Silence dropped over the table.

Shawn felt himself flush.

He couldn't believe Andrew had actually said that. And judging by the uncomfortable look that flashed over Andrew's face, he couldn't believe it, either. But then Andrew set his jaw, looking stubborn and determined: he might have regretted saying it, but he clearly wasn't taking it back.

Shawn bit his lip, unsure what to say. Andrew's words hit a bit too close to home. Of course no one here knew the nature of his relationship with Rutledge, but nevertheless, it made him feel embarrassed and humiliated.

Shawn hadn't completely come to terms with it himself, and now… he felt like a whore. It was ridiculous, but it was the first time he truly felt it. He hadn't felt like a whore when he sucked Rutledge's dick for money; he felt like a whore as he sat in this posh dining room with all these snobby people.

"Apologize." Rutledge. It was spoken in a quiet, steely voice, but everyone in the room heard him.

Andrew glared at Rutledge.

"Why would I? We all can see he's poor and fucking you for—"

"You will apologize," Rutledge said, his tone dangerously soft.

"Andrew, please," Vivian said, awkwardly. "That was uncalled for—"

"Apologize," Rutledge said again.

Joseph Rutledge said nothing, watching the exchange between his son and son-in-law like a hawk.

"It's all right," Shawn said lightly.

Rutledge ignored him and continued glowering at Andrew, who looked increasingly uncomfortable. "He will apologize or we're leaving."

Shawn thought it was an odd threat to make, because Andrew would be clearly delighted if they left, but Joseph Rutledge frowned. "Apologize, boy. No one insults my guests."

Except for you, Shawn thought, not without humor.

Andrew said stiffly, "My apologies if I offended anyone. It wasn't my intention."

Rutledge didn't look satisfied in the least, his body tense and eyes narrowed.

"If you must know," Shawn told Andrew. "I'm a student, and I work part-time as a waiter. Yes, Derek pays most of my bills. I'm not ashamed of that. I'm lucky to have such a supportive, dependable partner." He looked Andrew in the eye. "And if I 'spread my legs for him,' it has nothing to do with it, and it's definitely none of your business." Shawn raised his eyebrows. "I'm not sure why you even brought it up, Andrew. Unless you're envious."

He smiled as the asshole's face slowly turned red. Shawn didn't even mind the stunned, awkward silence that descended upon the room. He picked up his fork and started eating again, ignoring everyone.

He could feel Rutledge's gaze on him.

Shawn didn't turn his head.

Chapter Ten

Shawn spent a few hours playing with Emily and Bee after dinner.

When the twins were finally exhausted and fell asleep, Shawn returned to his—their—bedroom.

It was empty.

Unsure if he was relieved or disappointed, Shawn grabbed fresh clothes and took a long shower. He stood for a while with the water pouring over his naked body and thought of the fact that he was going to share a bed with Rutledge. All night.

Shawn looked down at his half-hard dick and sighed. This was all so confusing. Rutledge was a man. He was also one fucked up asshole. He couldn't possibly be excited about sharing a bed with him.

Annoyed with his body, Shawn dried himself, dressed, and stepped back into the bedroom.

At first, he thought Rutledge was still elsewhere.

Then he spotted a tall figure out on the balcony.

Slowly, Shawn made his way towards the door, slid it open, and stepped out into the night.

When the chilly air hit him, he shivered a little and wrapped his arms around himself to keep warm. It was still pretty warm for November, but it was not warm enough for one thin layer.

Rutledge had a cigarette in his hand. He didn't turn his head.

Shawn leaned against the balcony railings, mirroring Rutledge's posture. "He's really ill, you know."

He noticed the subtle stiffening of Rutledge's shoulders only because he was watching him closely.

"Yes," Rutledge said tonelessly. "He's dying."

Shawn couldn't say he was surprised.

"I'm sorry."

Shrugging, Rutledge took a long drag from his cigarette. "There's no love lost between us."

Shawn looked at the moon as it peeked out from the clouds. "When my parents died, they left huge debts. The house had to be sold to pay off creditors, so I ended up homeless, barely legal, and with two toddlers to care for. Sometimes I hate them. For dying, for being so irresponsible and putting me in this position." He felt his throat thicken and had to swallow the lump. Breathing in the clear night air, he tilted his face upward to feel the breeze brush across his skin. "But I miss them. So fucking much."

Rutledge didn't say anything.

Somewhere in the distance, an owl hooted.

"He's your dad," Shawn said.

Rutledge stubbed the cigarette out.

"I didn't bring you here so that you can lecture me about the importance of family." His voice was clipped. Irritated.

"No. You brought me here to annoy your dad and prove your point. Don't you think it's petty and nasty?"

"He's no victim. Dying doesn't make him less of a piece of shit."

"It doesn't," Shawn agreed.

"And you know nothing about our relationship."

"You're right: I know nothing. We've already established I'm just a dumb pretty boy."

Rutledge turned to him. Shawn could feel the heat of his glare even in the dark.

"You're incredibly annoying," Rutledge said before yanking Shawn to him and crushing their lips together.

Several minutes later, Shawn opened his eyes and said, "This is annoying, too. You're using my oral fixation thing against me."

Rutledge kissed him again, and everything went dizzy, hot, and overwhelming.

Some unidentifiable time later, Shawn opened his eyes again and found himself lying in bed. Naked. And Rutledge was licking his nipple.

"We aren't having sex," Shawn said.

"Of course we aren't," Rutledge agreed. He was naked, too.

Shawn's dazed gaze skimmed over his broad shoulders, densely muscled chest, and taut stomach, before lingering on his hard red cock. He felt his mouth water.

"No, seriously," Shawn tried again but bit his lip

when Rutledge wrapped a hand around his erection. God. "We aren't having sex."

Rutledge stroked Shawn's cock a few times before letting go and spreading Shawn's thighs.

Shawn tensed.

Rutledge stroked his inner thighs, his hands strong, and big, and so good—

"Don't even think about it," Shawn managed.

"Just lie back and enjoy, Wyatt."

Shawn laughed. "Right. Like I don't know what you really want. You want to stick your dick in me."

Rutledge's eyes seemed black as they met his. "I do want to 'stick my dick' in you. Before the night is over, you'll want me to stick my dick in you, too."

Shawn snorted, looking at Rutledge's thick cock. "There's no way in hell I'll let that thing anywhere near my ass."

"We'll see." Rutledge's finger pressed firmly against the spot behind Shawn's balls, making Shawn gasp. "I think you will. And you'll look good on my cock."

Shawn flushed. "Fuck you. You're such an asshole. Bossy and—"

"Stop pretending you don't like it." Rutledge's big hands stroked Shawn's thighs again. "You like having someone in charge of you. You like to not have to be responsible for once and just let go."

Shawn opened his mouth to protest but he couldn't deny it. His dick seemed to like Rutledge's bossiness a whole lot. "It doesn't mean I want your dick in my ass. I'm not even sure how that's supposed to feel good.

There's no way it'll fit."

"It'll fit, don't worry." Rutledge's eyes looked dazed with lust as they roamed over Shawn's naked body. "I must fuck you. The sooner, the better."

Shawn licked his lips. "I don't think—"

"Turn onto your stomach," Rutledge said.

"I—"

"Turn onto your stomach," Rutledge said again, in the tone of voice he used in classroom.

Shawn's cock twitched. He rolled over, closed his eyes, and told himself he could stop Rutledge any moment if things got too weird. He would.

Hands kneaded and stroked his ass before something wet and soft touched his buttock.

Shawn tensed. "Wait—"

"Relax, you'll like it. All straight boys like it." Rutledge chuckled darkly. "Don't worry, it won't make you gay."

Shawn found himself blushing. "Um, I had a shower, and I'm clean, but—"

"You have a beautiful ass." Rutledge bit his buttock. "I've wanted to do this to you for ages."

Rutledge's lips closed down around his hole and *sucked,* and Shawn's brain gave up the battle. Rutledge's tongue pressed forward, tracing around his hole before giving it a long lick, and Shawn moaned, his thighs spreading wider of their own volition. Christ, nothing should feel this good.

Soft, and slick, he felt Rutledge's tongue licking him, lapping at his hole with abandon. Then Rutledge's thumbs held him open to the assault.

Fuck. Rutledge's tongue worked into him slowly, giving soft jabs at his center, parting the muscle, coaxing it to relax, sliding inside. Eating him out. So filthy, so wrong, but Shawn made a noise that sounded suspiciously like a sob, rutting against the mattress, his cock rock hard and throbbing.

"More," he gasped, shifting his body until he was on his knees, legs spread and head hung low. The stubble on Rutledge's face scratched the soft flesh of his buttocks, intensifying the sensations and reminding him once again that it was a man licking his hole. It was his professor eating him out.

The thought sent a rush of blood to his cock and he whimpered, pushing back against Rutledge's mouth as Rutledge fucked him with his tongue. It wasn't enough. His hole felt oversensitive, clenching for something hard to grab hold of.

They moved together, that wicked tongue trying to get deeper into him with every forward thrust.

He was whimpering and shaking so badly, on edge and unable to come. He ached, and Rutledge's tongue wasn't big enough, couldn't get deep enough, and Shawn needed more. "More."

Rutledge pulled away from him, and then there were slick fingers massaging Shawn's entrance with a circular motion, and Shawn moaned. He was having trouble thinking, his body taking over and trying to impale itself on Rutledge's fingers. Rutledge pushed the fingers in—one, then another, scissoring them quickly before pulling them out again.

Panting, Shawn waited.

He heard the sound of a condom wrapper tearing open. It should have made him panic—what was about to happen—but he was past the point of freaking out. He was so empty. So hard.

Rutledge flipped him onto his back. Shoving a pillow under Shawn's hips, he lined himself up between his legs, his dark eyes glazed with desire.

Shawn willed himself to relax as the thick head of Rutledge's cock slowly started to stretch him. He felt himself pulled taut, burning, as Rutledge slowly pushed into him, Shawn's insides reluctantly giving way to the intrusion.

"Oh," Shawn breathed out when Rutledge was fully inside. He gripped Rutledge's arms, his thighs trembling. It hurt a little.

Rutledge took a deep breath in, his muscles rigid under Shawn's fingers. Rutledge's body was tense as hell, as though he was fighting for control.

Shawn's eyes fluttered shut, mouth falling open as he panted hotly. He was practically impaled on Rutledge's cock, pleasure chasing the pain as he was stretched to his limit. He felt so full, Rutledge's cock heavy inside him in all the right ways. It still ached, creating an exquisite agony that made his cock throb and leak against his stomach. The sensation of fullness was satisfying in a way he couldn't explain.

"I'm good," Shawn said, and to his surprise, he was. The intensity, the feeling of vulnerability was doing strange things to him, and he was melting, and he wanted—

Rutledge started moving.

Shawn could only open and close his mouth uselessly as the weird, intense pleasure started building up.

Rutledge's cock nudged against his prostate, hard, and Shawn cried out, fingers digging into Rutledge's shoulders. "Oh god, oh god," he muttered between unintelligible words and noises as Rutledge thrust in and out, fucking him in earnest now. It still hurt, but Shawn could only concentrate on the intense, maddening pleasure building up inside of him. He was aching all over, need pumping in him as Rutledge's cock buried deep in him, but not deep enough, never enough, and it was good, so good, so very good—

Tossing his head back, Shawn bit his lip as Rutledge practically bent him in half, directing his cock at an angle that made Shawn whimper.

Rutledge leaned down and started kissing him in time with his thrusts, his tongue delving deeply, and all Shawn could do was hold on and ride with the storm.

He completely lost track of time, his whole world narrowing to Rutledge—*Derek*—his hot mouth, his cock, his hands roaming all over Shawn's body. Shawn wasn't even speaking anymore, just taking it and moaning. His hole was twitching around Rutledge's cock as Rutledge pounded into him without restraint, kissing and biting Shawn's neck and shoulders. Shawn's dick was near bursting and he tried to touch himself, but Rutledge didn't let him.

Shawn could feel his belly tightening, feel his hole begin to pulse, throbbing down around the hard cock that continued to fuck him, never letting up, taking his breath and his sanity and his inhibitions.

Shawn groaned, digging his fingers into Rutledge's shoulders. "I can't—"

"You can." Rutledge gave a brutal thrust against Shawn's prostate, his fingers gripping Shawn's hips painfully. "Come on."

And Shawn came, his body shuddering as his orgasm ripped through him.

Rutledge slammed into him a few times before groaning and going very still on top of him.

Shawn lay limply under him, his breathing still erratic, his body quivering in aftershocks.

He felt himself drift off to sleep, feeling warm, good, and satisfied.

Chapter Eleven

When Shawn woke up, he was alone. Judging by the sunlight coming through the window, it was about eight in the morning.

Yawning, he sat up and stretched, trying to gather his thoughts.

Last night's events seemed bizarre and surreal. If his muscles didn't ache and his ass didn't hurt a little, he would have thought it was just a dream.

But it wasn't a dream.

He'd had real sex with Rutledge. He'd had Rutledge's cock in him.

Licking his lips, Shawn climbed out of the bed, wincing a little as the movement sent a fresh wave of dull pain through his ass, and walked to the mirror.

He was covered in bruises.

Shawn stared at the finger-shaped bruises on his hips and thighs and tried to decide whether he was freaking out or not. He was, a bit, but not because of the whole gay thing. Sure, he had never expected to have sex with a man, but gay sex in itself didn't bother him that much—at least not to the point of panicking and being hysterical. His parents were gone, and his best friend was bi, so there was no one to judge him—no one he cared about.

What did bother Shawn was the fact that he'd had sex with *Rutledge*. It wasn't in the deal.

Sure, Rutledge had been pretty bossy and determined to fuck him, but Shawn could have easily refused. Could have easily stopped him. But he hadn't. *That* freaked him out.

Not to mention the intensity of sex had been almost scary. Scary good.

Biting his lip, Shawn ran a finger over the bruise on his hip. His skin tingled.

The bathroom door suddenly opened, and Shawn jumped a little.

Rutledge stepped out of the bathroom, buttoning up his shirt. He came to a halt at the sight of Shawn, and Shawn had to suppress the urge to cover himself with his hands. He forced his body to relax, telling himself not to be ridiculous. He had nothing Rutledge hadn't seen already last night.

Something flashed across Rutledge's face before it closed off, his features becoming hard and distant. "How much do you want?"

"What?"

"How much do you want for last night?"

Shawn sucked in a sharp breath. "How much do I want?" he repeated.

Rutledge walked to the desk and picked up his cell phone. "Yes. Name your price."

Shawn stared at his wide back. "Price."

"Yes, price," Rutledge said, an edge of irritation creeping into his voice. "What's so hard to understand?"

His stomach clenching, Shawn picked up his discarded boxers and slipped them on, ignoring the discomfort in his ass.

He wanted a shower—he felt dirty—but he didn't want to remain naked and vulnerable.

"Five thousand," he said. That had to make Rutledge angry, right?

A pause.

"Fine."

Apparently not.

Shawn would have laughed, except the knot in his stomach rose, becoming a tight lump in his throat and making him vaguely sick.

Without a word, he made his way to the bathroom and shut the door very quietly.

Leaning back against it, Shawn closed his eyes.

The door was cold against his skin.

* * *

A long, hot shower cleared his head.

By the time Shawn emerged out of the bathroom, he knew what to do, but Rutledge was gone.

Shawn was about to call him when he noticed Rutledge's cell phone on the desk. Sighing, Shawn went to check on the twins, but they were still asleep, so he decided to go find Rutledge. The sooner he got it over with, the better.

After about fifteen minutes of wandering, Shawn finally admitted he had no clue where he was anymore. This wing of the mansion was completely unfamiliar to him, and he couldn't find any servants to tell him where Rutledge was.

The mansion was almost eerily quiet. The place was luxurious, but it felt like a museum, not someone's home. Shawn wondered what it would have been like to grow up here, and a chill ran up his spine.

Entering yet another room, Shawn froze upon seeing Joseph Rutledge seated behind a huge desk.

"Sorry," Shawn said, taking a step back. "I didn't mean to—"

"As a matter of fact, I wanted to speak to you, Mr. Wyatt."

"Me?" Shawn looked at him warily but stepped back into the room and closed the door.

Joseph's thick gray eyebrows drew together. "Indeed. Take a seat."

Shawn sat down in the chair opposite the old man and waited.

The silence stretched as they eyed each other.

Once again, Shawn was taken aback by how much Joseph Rutledge and his son resembled each other. It appeared the men in this family aged very well. This was what Rutledge would look like in thirty or forty years.

Not that Shawn would see it.

"Mr. Wyatt," Joseph Rutledge said at last when Shawn refused to drop his gaze. "For how long have you been in this unnatural relationship with my son?"

Shawn had to remind himself that Joseph Rutledge was very ill. He shouldn't be getting into arguments with a dying man. "Less than a month, sir."

"That makes it easier." Joseph Rutledge picked up a pen and wrote something on a piece of paper before sliding it across the desk to Shawn. "I believe this would be a fair compensation for ending your association with my son."

Shawn glanced at the paper and then stared at it.

"Wow, I'm flattered you value me so highly," he said and stood up. "Thanks, but no thanks."

"You're a fool, boy," said the old man with a disdainful look. "He will throw you away in a few weeks at most. He always does."

"How do you know that? You hadn't seen him in fifteen years."

Joseph sneered. "He might not live here anymore, but it changes nothing. I know everything about him. Every toy he had and threw away. Granted, there were a few persistent ones, but everybody has a price."

When his meaning registered, Shawn felt sick to his stomach. "You're sick," he whispered. "Does he know you paid his lovers off?"

Joseph raised an eyebrow.

"Of course he does. He's my son. He's no fool—except for his foolish insistence that he is homosexual."

Shaking his head, Shawn stood up and headed to the door. There was no reasoning with this man.

When he opened the door, Joseph's voice stopped him,

"Name your price, Mr. Wyatt. Everything has a price."

"Some things don't." Shawn walked out.

Everybody has a price.

So this was what Joseph Rutledge had taught his son.

Shawn wasn't sure who he pitied more at this moment: Rutledge, his father, or himself.

Chapter Twelve

He finally found Rutledge on the terrace half an hour later.

"I'm going home," Shawn said.

Rutledge's back stiffened. He turned around, a cigarette in his hand.

Strange. Until yesterday, Shawn had thought he didn't smoke at all.

Rutledge took a long drag, studying him with an unreadable expression. "Why? We're supposed to leave tomorrow."

"I talked to your father."

For a moment, Rutledge went very still before a sardonic smile appeared on his face. "How much did he offer you?"

"A lot. Only an idiot would refuse."

Rutledge turned away. "Congratulations. The easiest money you've ever made."

Shawn eyed his straight back. "Well, we've already established I'm dumb, didn't we?"

A pause.

Rutledge let out a laugh. "You should have taken the money, Wyatt."

"I don't like him."

Rutledge turned around again and crushed his cigarette with his shoe. "No one likes him. It's not a good enough reason not to accept his money. We know it would have made no difference."

"We know it, but he doesn't." Shawn cocked his head. "Are you really okay with me accepting his money? He thinks I'm your boyfriend."

Rutledge's lips twisted. "My father has been paying my boyfriends off ever since I was fifteen. You wouldn't have been the first. The old man's stubborn enough to think I'll marry a nice little girl if he puts an end to every relationship I try to have. Though I'm a bit surprised this time. Usually he bothers only if the guy lasts more than a month—which doesn't happen that often."

Shawn stared at him. "You can't mean all of them accepted his money."

"No. Not all of them. But most."

There was a bland mask of indifference on Rutledge's face, and Shawn had to curl his hands into fists and look away, trying to shake off the urge to touch him.

"You said he reminded you of me," Rutledge said. "But he takes it to a whole new level. He doesn't know when to stop."

"Yeah," Shawn murmured. "He's a narrow-minded, self-absorbed, high-handed asshole, and he fucked you up. But it doesn't excuse you when you act like a dick. And if you keep being so insensitive and keep treating people like pawns, you'll turn into him. Do you want that?"

"I didn't bring you along so you could psychoanalyze me."

"No, you didn't bring me along for that," Shawn said, his voice quiet. "But I'm done."

Rutledge's gaze sharpened. "What?"

"I'm a bit sick of being treated like a cheap whore by your family."

"I wouldn't call you cheap," Rutledge said, his voice clipped.

Shawn laughed softly. "Okay, maybe I deserve it. I needed money and wasn't proud enough to say no, but I'm kind of sick of it now. This is it, Professor."

He turned to leave, but Rutledge crossed the distance between them in a few strides and grabbed his arm. "You can't leave. We have a deal."

Shawn looked at him, ignoring Rutledge's painful grip on his arm. "We had a deal. I'm ending it now. I think I more than earned the money you paid me for this trip. You can keep the money for last night's sex. On the house."

He tried to yank his hand free, but Rutledge's grip only tightened. "You can't just decide to leave."

"Why not? Why do you even mind?" He smiled brightly. "Didn't you say you get bored of straight guys after you fuck them? Lucky for you, then."

Rutledge's lips pressed into a thin line. His grasp loosened.

Yanking his arm free, Shawn strode away.

* * *

By the time Shawn managed to dress the girls and get them out of the house, Rutledge's car was waiting for them.

Shawn stared out the window for most of the drive, feigning interest in the scenery passing by. The twins were doing all the talking.

He didn't look at Rutledge, but the tension in the air between them was palpable, and the sheer amount of anger and frustration was overwhelming. Shawn wasn't even sure why. It wasn't like Rutledge was his ex or something; it wasn't like they had been dating; there was no reason this should affect him. He had sucked his professor's dick for a few weeks(granted, not something he was proud of), had been dragged along to annoy Joseph Rutledge and got paid handsomely for it. He was finally done whoring himself out, and now he had a few months to find a better job without worrying about the bills every day. So everything was fine. Great. Fantastic, actually.

Yet it was such a relief when the car finally stopped in front of his building.

It took Shawn a few minutes to get the girls out of the car. Rutledge already had Shawn's suitcase out.

"Thanks, I'll take it now," Shawn said, without looking at him.

"Don't be silly," Rutledge said, walking toward the building. "You don't have three hands."

"The girls don't need me to carry them. They're old enough to walk."

Rutledge ignored him, of course. Of course.

"We can walk," Emily confirmed.

"But I wanna be carried," Bee said.

Shawn glared at Rutledge's back and picked up the girls. "You don't even know where you're going."

"I know your address. I'm capable of figuring out where your apartment is."

Scowling, Shawn could only follow him.

When they reached his apartment, Shawn hesitated. He didn't want Rutledge to see it. It wasn't that he was embarrassed of it—fine, maybe he was embarrassed of it.

He opened the door and ushered the girls inside before closing it and turning to Rutledge.

Rutledge set the suitcase down, his expression stony.

"I…" Shawn said, shifting slightly on his feet. "I'll see you around, I guess."

Rutledge nodded curtly. But he didn't move.

Shawn cleared his throat, hooking his thumbs in his pockets and rocking back on his heels. "Thanks, by the way."

"For what?"

"For helping me figure out I'm not straight."

"What?" Rutledge said, almost without inflection.

"Yeah. In case you couldn't tell, I liked having sex with a man." Shawn smiled faintly. "I didn't expect it, but I did. A lot. So… I have more options now. I guess I should thank you for that."

"Options," Rutledge said.

"Yep." Shawn rubbed the back of his neck. "I can date guys too now."

Something changed in Rutledge's expression, but it was gone before Shawn could figure out what it was.

"You can," Rutledge agreed, pushing his hands into the pockets of his jacket.

Damn. Why was it so weird, and awkward—and whatever the hell it was?

Shawn was sure he wasn't imagining the tension, the frustration in the air, yet Rutledge's face betrayed nothing. And it pissed Shawn off. He wanted to shake him. He wanted to shock him.

So he said, "You know, I actually can't wait to find out if sex with other guys will be different. It's all new and very exciting."

Rutledge looked aside for a moment before a smile formed on his face. "Are you trying to make me jealous, Wyatt? I don't do jealousy. Jealousy is for insecure men with small dicks and low self-esteem. And you have to care to be jealous. I don't."

Shawn bristled at the implications. "Why would I want to make you jealous? I don't like you. Your family is horrible, you're an ass, you're beyond fucked up, and you're a commitment-phobe. And you don't like children—which is obviously a big deal for me. You're everything I don't want."

"Good." Rutledge glared at him.

Their gazes clashed and a rush of carnal hunger slammed into Shawn with a force that stole his breath.

His fingers trembling, Shawn found the doorknob behind him and stumbled into the apartment.

Shutting the door, Shawn leaned against it, breathing hard.

Fuck.

Chapter Thirteen

"I don't get it," Christian said a week later, looking at him from across the table in the campus cafeteria. "Why is he such an asshole to you? I mean, he's always an asshole, but lately he's been a super asshole when it comes to you."

Shawn suppressed a sigh. Christian was right, of course. Rutledge had been treating him like shit the entire week. Not that it came as a complete surprise.

"Seriously, did you kill his cat? Or—or leave a bloody chicken on his doorstep or something?" Christian shook his head. "There has to be some explanation. It's getting ridiculous. People are starting to talk."

Shawn's coffee cup paused halfway to his mouth. "Talk?"

"Never mind." Christian grimaced, looking a bit uncomfortable. "Just some stupid rumors."

"What rumors, Chris?"

Christian took a sip from his coffee. "Some think it's suspicious that Rutledge didn't give you a failing midterm grade."

Shawn stopped breathing. "What?"

"Some say you blackmailed him into giving you a passing grade. I told you it's stupid."

Shawn relaxed, leaning back in his chair. "Yeah. Stupid."

"Actually, it is a bit strange, don't you think? I thought he'd fail you for sure. But he didn't, and now he's a total asshole to you. The whole thing is weird." Christian gave him a probing look. "You sure you aren't hiding something from me?"

Shawn felt a pang of guilt. He took a gulp of his coffee and looked at his cup. "Maybe."

"All right, spill," Christian said, training his eyes on him.

Shawn began tracing the rim of the cup with his finger, following its shape. "I… remember the advice you gave me? On Rutledge?"

Christian chuckled. "You mean flirting?"

"Rutledge didn't give me a passing grade because he took pity on me, Chris."

Christian's eyebrows furrowed; then his jaw dropped. "No way. You actually followed my advice?"

Shawn grimaced. "Not exactly." He looked down at the sandwich on his plate and pulled at the cheese sticking out at the edges. "I did more than flirting."

A clang made him look up. Christian had dropped his fork and was now looking at him with wide eyes. "You're kidding."

"I wish."

Christian glanced around and then moved his chair closer. "So what did he make you do?"

"What do you think? Not a hand-job for sure."

"Holy shit. You sucked him off?"

Shawn nodded curtly.

Christian let out a short laugh. "Wow, I never thought you'd actually flirt with him, much less... So, what was it like? I mean, were you grossed out?" He sipped his coffee.

Shawn was tempted to say yes. It would have made everything simpler. But he couldn't bring himself to lie.

"No," Shawn said. "It was okay. Even the first time."

Christian choked on his coffee and started coughing.

"The first time?" he said when the coughing finally subsided. "You mean you did it more than once? Is he still forcing you to do it for a grade?"

Shawn wondered whether whoring himself out for a grade was better than whoring himself out for money. He wasn't sure. "Look… I don't really want to talk about it. Yeah, it'd been going on for a few weeks, but the important thing is, it's over now. I ended the deal."

"But did you, you know… did you fuck him?"

"Yeah," Shawn said, struggling to keep his voice casual. "I fucked him. Well, he fucked me."

Christian grinned, brown eyes dancing with mischief. "How was he? Any good?"

Smiling crookedly, Shawn shook his head. "Come on, do we have to talk about it?"

"Of course we have to talk about it! You had sex with Rutledge! Rutledge!"

"Hush," Shawn hissed, glancing around.

"I don't want to talk about it. Nothing to talk about. It didn't—it didn't suck, but obviously I'm glad the whole thing is over."

He felt Christian's eyes on him, unusually serious and assessing. Shawn fidgeted under his scrutiny. "What?"

"Then why is he so pissed at you if it's over?" Christian said, drumming his fingers on the table.

Shawn had an idea why, but it wasn't something he wanted to think about. "No idea."

Christian gave him a skeptical look, but didn't press any further and looked down at his cup. He fell silent, a distant, thoughtful expression on his face.

Shawn eyed his friend. Come to think of it, Christian had been a bit distracted all day. "Something wrong?"

Christian looked up. "Not really. Just…you know Mila?"

"Mila?"

"The girl in Rutledge's class? Very pretty, curvy, dark hair?"

Shawn shrugged. "It's a big class. Can't say I remember her. So what about her?"

"She invited me for a threesome."

Shawn raised his eyebrows. "And what's the problem? It's not like you've never done threesomes before." There was very little Christian hadn't done, actually. His friend got so many lewd offers sometimes it got silly. The guy didn't even have to try. If Christian wasn't so damn likable, all guys would hate him.

"The problem is her boyfriend," Christian said.

"What about him? You know him?"

Christian hesitated. "Not exactly. But I've seen him around. He always picks her up after school."

Shawn snorted a laugh, finally realizing who his friend was talking about. "The straight guy you've been crushing on for ages?"

"Come on, I don't have a crush on him," Christian said with a lopsided smile. "I don't even know his name."

Shawn gave him a look that said, *Please*. "Yup, you don't have a crush on him. You just stare and drool whenever you see him."

"I don't."

"You do."

Christian laughed. "Fine. Maybe. Just a tiny one. But come on, who doesn't? All girls stare at him and drool whenever he comes. The guy is ridiculously good-looking."

"So what's the problem?" Shawn said. "Shouldn't you be

happy you'll get to have sex with him?"

Christian looked at him like he was an idiot. "He's straight. It's not going to be that kind of threesome. We'll just share his girlfriend; that's all. Maybe I'm wrong, but I got the feeling the threesome is entirely Mila's idea—she always flirts with me, and I don't think he even knows I exist. I don't think the guy is all too happy about her inviting me to join them. I don't know… I get the impression he's the possessive type."

"A tiny crush, yup," Shawn teased. "Very tiny."

Christian's ears turned red. "Oh, shut it. Anyway, that's the problem: I'm not sure this threesome is a good idea. The guy will probably hate my guts for touching his girl."

"Then tell her you can't do it."

"I already told her I would." Christian gave him a sheepish look. "Couldn't resist the chance to see him naked."

Shawn shook his head. "You're hopeless, man."

Christian grinned. "At least I'm not fucking Professor Asshole. Come on, tell me he has a tiny dick! It would make my day!"

Shawn rolled his eyes, shaking his head. "He doesn't have a tiny dick. And I'm not fucking him anymore. We're done." He lifted his cup and brought it to his lips, avoiding Christian's eyes. He thought about the way Rutledge had looked at him back in class: angry and so damn intense it made him instantly hard. He thought about how he'd spent half of the class fantasizing about dropping to his knees before Rutledge and sucking his dick, right there, in front of all other students. He thought about his other fantasies: how he wanted to climb into Rutledge's lap, shut him up with kisses and then get Rutledge's cock inside of him—

"You all right?" Christian said. "You look flushed."

Shawn forced a smile. "Yeah. I'm fine."

Just peachy.

Chapter Fourteen

Shawn's cousin Sage lived in a less than safe part of the city. It was partly why Shawn didn't see him much. The other reason was that his cousin had been weird as hell after he was released from prison six months ago: he seemed depressed and distant, like he wasn't even there. At first Shawn attributed it to his aunt's death—she had died while Sage was still in prison—but it didn't seem to be the case. Instead of getting better, his cousin seemed only more depressed as time went on. Shawn was worried about him, of course, but truth be told, he had more pressing problems to think about and didn't have time to visit his cousin.

But since he'd had to drop the kids at Mrs. Hawkins's place before his night shift, Shawn decided to make a small detour and find out how Sage was doing.

His cousin greeted him with a grin. "Hey, come on in," he said, opening the door wider.

It took Shawn a moment to recover from his surprise.

"You look good," he said, patting him on the shoulder and entering the apartment.

Sage looked great actually; he'd always been the better-looking one out of the two of them.

They might share their moms' blond hair and blue eyes, but that was where the similarities ended. His cousin's features were far more delicate—hell, downright exquisite. If Christian had seen Sage, he would never call Shawn the princess anymore.

It actually made Shawn wonder, and not for the first time, whether something… had been done to his cousin in prison. If the rumors about what happened in prison were true, with a face like this… Shawn shuddered.

"How are the girls?" Sage asked, pulling him away from his thoughts.

"Good. I have the night shift tonight, so I just dropped them at their babysitter's."

Sage sat on the couch, cross-legged, and patted the place next to him.

Removing his jacket, Shawn took the seat. "I can't really stay," he said, glancing at his watch. "Or I'll be late for work. I just wanted to check on you and see how you were doing—"

The door opened and a man walked into the apartment.

Seeing Shawn, he stopped and stared.

Shawn stared back. The man was tall and pretty handsome, clearly of Hispanic descent.

"Who is that?" the guy asked.

"It's my cousin, Shawn," Sage said, rather defensively. "Shawn, it's Xavier."

Shawn waited for an explanation, but there was none.

But when Xavier walked over, tipped Sage's head up and kissed him, no explanations were needed anymore.

The kiss went on and on, and Shawn could only stare. He'd been pretty sure Sage was completely straight.

Well, apparently not.

His cousin actually moaned, and Shawn looked away, beyond uncomfortable. He stood up and cleared his throat.

"Um, I'd better go." He chuckled. "You're clearly fine."

Behind him, the kissing stopped.

"Look," Sage said, sounding embarrassed. "I—"

"You don't have to explain anything," Shawn said quickly and headed to the door. "I'll go."

"Wait," Sage said. "It's dark already. It's not safe to walk alone around here. Xavier will drive you home."

"I will?" Xavier murmured.

"No, it really isn't necessary—"

"He will," Sage said.

"I guess I will," Xavier said. He gave Sage a short, hard kiss. "You'd better be naked and ready when I'm back, Blue Eyes."

Flushing, Sage pushed Xavier to the door. "I'll come over next week," he told Shawn. "I haven't seen the girls in ages."

Shawn nodded and put on his jacket.

Xavier moved past him. "Let's go. What was your name again?"

"Shawn," he said, not sure how to talk to the guy.

"Where do you live?"

Shawn told him, and Xavier led him to a very old, rusty Ford Pinto. Shawn looked at it warily. "Are you sure this thing is safe?"

"No," the guy said, getting in the driver's seat.

"That's… not very reassuring."

"Did you want me to lie?" Xavier said with a hint of impatience, clearly eager to get it over with and go back to his cousin.

Shawn got in the car, and they took off.

"There's no seatbelt," Shawn muttered. "Why am I not surprised?"

Xavier didn't deign to reply.

"So," Shawn said after a while. "Are you my cousin's boyfriend or something?"

"Or something," Xavier said.

"I thought he was straight."

Xavier just laughed, as though he had said something funny.

"But I'm glad he has someone, you know," Shawn said. "I was worried about him. He was depressed after he got out of prison."

"Really?" Xavier murmured.

"Yeah. I hope I'm wrong, but I think… I think someone did something to him in prison."

"You're not wrong: I did."

Shawn opened his mouth and closed it without saying a word. He digested the information for a few moments. "You're an ex-convict?"

"Yep."

Great. He was in a rusty Ford Pinto, without a seatbelt on, and with an ex-convict at the wheel.

"What were you in prison for?"

"Killed eight people at a mall."

Shawn snorted a laugh. "You don't actually expect me to believe that, do you?"

"Your cousin did, for a long time."

Shawn smiled, shaking his head. Sage was a bit naive. Even though he was younger than his cousin, Shawn often felt like he was the older one. "So what did you really do?"

"Manslaughter. Got drunk, got into a bar fight, someone died."

A shiver of unease ran down Shawn's spine. He couldn't imagine what this guy and Sage had in common, but his cousin was clearly happy. That was the important thing, wasn't it?

They were quiet for the rest of the drive.

"Thanks," Shawn said when the car finally stopped in front of his building. To his surprise, Xavier got out, as well. Shawn chuckled. "No one will attack me here. You don't have to—"

"Sage told me to get you home. I'll get you home." Xavier was looking over Shawn's shoulder. "Someone's watching us. You know that guy?"

Shawn turned around and froze. Rutledge got out of his Mercedes and strode toward them.

"Yeah, I know him," Shawn said.

"He looks pissed," Xavier murmured.

Shawn let out a laugh. "He pretty much always looks pissed." He cringed—it came out almost affectionate—and Xavier shot him a sharp, assessing look.

Rutledge came to a halt.

"Hey," Shawn said, unsure.

Rutledge gave him the glare he'd been giving him the entire week before looking at Xavier with such a look of disdain that it would make anyone feel two inches tall. "Who is that?"

Xavier seemed unfazed, even amused.

"Xavier Otero," he said with a nice smile, stepping closer to Shawn and putting a hand on his shoulder. "I was just giving Shawn a ride." Shawn inhaled sharply at the dirty undertone in his voice.

Rutledge clearly didn't miss it, either. His shoulders tensed up and his gaze raked over Shawn, as if looking for evidence, before shifting to Xavier's car. A sneer twisted his lips. "I hope the ride was comfortable."

Xavier's eyes flickered to Rutledge's Mercedes. He shrugged lazily. "I don't need a flashy car for that."

"Nicely done, guys, that wasn't passive-aggressive at all," Shawn said, suppressing the urge to facepalm.

He looked at Xavier. "Don't take it personally—he's nasty to everyone. And you"—Shawn looked at Rutledge—"tone it down a bit. He's an ex-convict, not your student."

"He's a criminal?" In a blink of an eye, Shawn was yanked away from Xavier and pushed behind Rutledge's back.

"Hey! Are you out of—"

"Get in your car and drive away," Rutledge told Xavier. "Stay away from him or I'll make sure you'll be back in your cell in no time."

Xavier narrowed his eyes, his amusement gone. "You think you can threaten me?"

"Oh, for fuck's sake!" Shawn stepped between the two men, putting a hand on Rutledge's chest. He glared at them. Arrogant idiots. "You." He looked at Xavier. "Thanks for the ride, but please go home and fuck my cousin. No one's threatening you—it's just Rutledge's charming personality. Go."

Xavier nodded stiffly, climbed into his car and started it.

When the car disappeared out of sight, Shawn turned to Rutledge. "And you. What happened to jealousy being 'for men with small dicks and low self-esteem?'"

"Nothing," Rutledge said testily. "Are you stupid? Do you know what criminals like him do to pretty boys like you in prison? Men like him aren't used to asking."

Shawn chuckled. "Are you worried for me? I'm touched. Careful, or I'll start thinking you actually give a damn."

Rutledge glowered at him but said nothing.

"What are you even doing here?" Shawn asked. Belatedly, he realized his hand was still on Rutledge's chest and was stroking it. Quickly, he removed it and shoved it into the pocket of his jacket. He glanced at Rutledge's car. "Wait, were you waiting for me?"

"Yes."

"Why? You could have called if you wanted to talk. You have my number."

"I don't. I erased it."

Shawn's eyebrows flew up. "Why? Did it bother you?"

A muscle twitched at Rutledge's temple. "Because I had no need for it."

"Then why are you here?"

Rutledge's lips pressed together, his eyes boring into Shawn. "I'm here to warn you."

"Warn me?"

"Yes, to warn you. Your performance in my class continues to be terrible—"

"Because you've been absolutely brutal!"

"—so don't expect me to pass you only because of your pretty face, and lips, and eyes, and—" Rutledge cut himself off and glared at Shawn, as if it was his fault he'd just said what he said. "My point is, you won't get special treatment, Wyatt."

Shawn leaned toward his lips and whispered harshly, "And you came all the way here just to tell me that? I call bullshit."

Their breathing mixed, both swift and strained, the only sound in Shawn's ears.

Christ, Shawn couldn't stand it anymore. He was trembling, aching—

When Rutledge crushed their lips together, the first thing Shawn felt was relief. God, finally. And then everything else faded away; there were big hands on his nape, a firm body against his, and lips, hot and searing—

so good—and Shawn was moaning, trying to kiss him harder, take him deeper.

He had no idea how much time had passed when his cell phone went off in the pocket of his jacket.

With a sigh of frustration, Shawn tore his lips away and answered it.

"Yeah?" he managed, fingers clenched in Rutledge's sweater as the man kissed his face and his neck. God, his lips seemed to burn Shawn's skin.

"Where the hell are you?" Bill, the manager of the restaurant. Fuck. "You're almost late for your shift!"

"Sorry, give me fifteen minutes—"

"Five!" Bill hung up.

Shawn pushed Rutledge away. "Need to go. I'm late for work."

He walked away quickly, his legs still weak and his body aching with want. "Idiot," he muttered. He should have told Xavier to take him straight to work. Hell, he shouldn't have gone to Sage's place at all after he'd dropped the twins at Mrs. Hawkins's. And he definitely shouldn't have spent minutes sucking Rutledge's tongue.

Tires screeched and a familiar Mercedes pulled up beside him. The car door flew open.

"Get in," Rutledge said. "I'll give you a ride."

Shawn hesitated, but what the hell. He really was running late. Pointless stubbornness was stupid.

He got in and told Rutledge the address of the restaurant. Sometimes he got assigned to the restaurant at the other end of the city, but luckily for Shawn, tonight it was the one close to his place.

Neither of them spoke during the short drive. Shawn leaned back against the seat and closed his eyes as he fought for control.

Thankfully, it only took about five minutes to reach the restaurant.

"Thanks," Shawn muttered, without looking at the other man, and opened the door.

Rutledge caught his arm.

Shawn took a shaky breath before turning to Rutledge.

Dark eyes looked at him grimly.

"Okay," Shawn said. "But this is the last time, got it?"

He leaned toward Rutledge, buried his fingers in his hair and gave him a deep, wet kiss. Rutledge accepted the kiss passively, but Shawn could feel his body vibrate with tension, and it made Shawn achingly hard.

The cell phone went off again.

Sighing, Shawn pulled away and whispered, "This is stupid. We both know it." He wiped his lips. "Let's just pretended this never happened, okay?"

Rutledge said nothing—just looked at Shawn with dark, hungry eyes.

And god, Shawn wanted to kiss him again. Badly.

Swearing through his teeth, he practically jumped out of the car.

Chapter Fifteen

Shawn was walking to his last class of the day when he saw Rutledge walking the other way.

His steps faltered for a moment before he averted his gaze and continued walking, determined to ignore him.

Except Rutledge didn't let him.

He grabbed Shawn's arm as they were passing each other. "A word, Mr. Wyatt."

Shawn wet his lips, his heart pounding. He looked straight in front of him. "I don't think we have anything to talk about, Professor."

The grasp on his hand tightened. "A word."

Shawn glanced around. "Let go. You're attracting attention."

Rutledge removed his hand and bit out, "Follow me."

"I have a class in a few minutes."

"I'll write you a note," Rutledge threw over his shoulder before walking away.

"That's abuse of power," Shawn grumbled but did follow him.

Rutledge led him into a classroom at the end of the hall. It was empty.

Shawn closed the door. "Look, this is—"

Rutledge slammed him against the wall and crushed their lips together.

Goddammit, not this again. But he was already kissing back and gasping into Rutledge's mouth.

The kiss was messy and needy, Rutledge pressing against him as though he was trying to embed him in the wall.

Shawn whined when the kiss ended as suddenly as it began.

Rutledge buried his face against the side of Shawn's throat, breathing deeply, his body tense as hell. "I want to fuck you." Rutledge sucked hard on the side of his neck, his hands kneading Shawn's ass and pushing their crotches together. "Need to fuck you again."

Shawn closed his eyes, trying to think, trying to remember how to breathe because it didn't seem like he was getting any oxygen to his brain and all his blood seemed to have drained into his cock and his head was blissfully empty. He couldn't for the life of him remember why it was such a bad idea—

"Why would Shawn be here—Oh."

Shawn froze. Rutledge went very still, his lips still on Shawn's neck.

Then they both turned their heads.

Christian stood in the half-open doorway, his mouth agape.

"He's not here," he said loudly, stepped back, and shut the door.

His face hot, Shawn sighed. "I should go."

But he didn't move.

Rutledge leaned his forehead against the wall next to Shawn's head. His hands were still gripping Shawn's hips, his thumbs on the bare skin of Shawn's lower stomach.

"This is all your fault," he said, his voice terse.

Shawn huffed, buried his hand in Rutledge's hair and tugged. "How is this my fault?"

"You shouldn't have decided to leave early," Rutledge said irritably, placing greedy, open-mouthed kisses on Shawn's neck. "If you hadn't done that, I would have fucked you a few more times until it got boring enough."

"Charming," Shawn said dryly—or rather, tried to, but his voice came out a little breathy.

Rutledge lifted his head from his neck. His pupils were completely blown as his gaze alternated between Shawn's eyes and mouth. "I'll come to your place tonight and we will fuck." That wasn't a question.

Shawn wet his lips. "Already forgot about the twins?"

Wrong answer. He should have refused outright.

Rutledge stared at his lips, his thumbs stroking Shawn's bare stomach. "Aren't kids supposed to go to sleep early?"

"I— I can't leave them alone. What if they wake up?"

"We'll be quiet."

Shawn wasn't sure he could be quiet. Not when he already had to swallow back moans just from having Rutledge's hands on his stomach.

"But—"

"I'll come tonight," Rutledge said firmly. "And we'll fuck."

He started leaning in to kiss Shawn again, but stopped, looked away, and stalked out of the room.

Shawn banged his head against the wall and had to wait for a while until his arousal faded and he could think—and move—again.

"How very nice of you to deign us with your presence, Mr. Wyatt," Professor Travis said when he entered the classroom. "Only twenty minutes late."

"I'm sorry, Professor," Shawn said, trying not to squirm under her sharp gaze. Professor Travis had never particularly liked him, but her class was actually one of his best, so she usually had no reason to criticize him. Until now.

"Do you have any explanation, Wyatt?"

Shawn rubbed the back of his neck. "Actually, yes. Professor Rutledge had an urgent task for me. He told me to apologize to you on his behalf. He's the reason I'm late."

The woman's eyebrows flew up. "Professor Rutledge?"

"Yep," Shawn said, trying hard not to laugh. He couldn't imagine Rutledge apologizing for anything, much less to this woman. "I'm really sorry for my tardiness, but if you have a problem with it, you'll have to take it up with Professor Rutledge."

Like hell she would.

Professor Travis still looked puzzled but nodded. "Very well. Sit down, Wyatt."

Shawn headed to his usual seat next to Christian.

"An urgent task, huh?" Christian murmured as soon as Shawn took his seat. "Like sucking his dick?"

Shawn felt himself blush. "Come on—"

"Look," Christian said quietly, his brown eyes looking at him intently. "I'm not judging. But you shouldn't have lied. It's over, my ass."

Shawn winced. "I really thought it was over, I swear. And it is. But…"

"But?"

Sighing, Shawn murmured, "I'm kind of really bad at thinking with my head when he puts his tongue in my mouth."

Christian stared at him for a short while before shaking his head slowly. "This is so weird, man. I mean, this isn't even some random guy we're talking about. It's *Rutledge!*"

"I know. I know it's weird, and stupid, and totally crazy and pointless. He's everything I don't want, but at the same time… Shit, it's fucking with my mind."

"But you still want him."

"Yeah," Shawn said.

"So what are you going to do about it?"

"He thinks if we fuck a few more times, it's bound to get boring." Shawn leaned back in his chair, running a hand over his face. "He'd better be right."

He'd better be.

Chapter Sixteen

The girls fell asleep at nine in the evening, just after Shawn returned from work.

After that, Shawn spent an hour trying to make the shabby apartment look semi-presentable. At last, he gave up on it as a lost cause and took a quick shower. Putting on a pair of old blue shorts, Shawn was drying himself off when there was a quiet knock on the door.

Barefoot, Shawn tiptoed to the door and opened it.

Rutledge's gaze immediately dropped down to his bare chest, his nipples, his belly button before settling on the shorts that were riding low on his hips.

Shawn cleared his throat quietly and Rutledge looked at his face.

In the semi-darkness of the room it was hard to read his expression.

Shawn pressed a finger to his lips and pointed to the girls' bed.

Rutledge nodded curtly.

Shawn took his hand, pulled him inside, and locked the door.

Then he led Rutledge to his bedroom.

It was the only bedroom in the apartment. When they had just moved in, Shawn had intended to make it the children's room, but it was cold and damp, so he'd ended up taking it himself.

The room was also small and devoid of any furniture besides the narrow bed and his desk. Shawn would have felt more embarrassed if Rutledge was actually looking around, but he didn't seem to be interested in his surroundings as he quietly shut the door and stared at Shawn in the dim light of the lamp.

Rutledge started silently undressing.

Shawn's heart beat faster and he could actually hear his own breathing, uneven and shaky. He stood still and watched, his skin warm, his cock hard and heavy in his shorts.

At last, Rutledge was naked. Looking completely unselfconscious, he walked to the bed, sat down and patted his knee, tension rolling off him in waves. His erection stood long and thick from a thatch of dark hair at his groin.

Shawn tore his gaze away, slipped out of his shorts and stepped to Rutledge.

He hesitated.

His eyes hooded, Rutledge took his arm and jerked him into his lap.

The rest was a blur of heated kisses and touches, and so much skin. Shawn had never felt so out of control with want, unable to think, unable to do anything but feel and want.

When he finally sank onto Rutledge's slick cock, the

profound relief was overwhelming. He groaned. The fullness, the intimacy was maddening and scary in its intensity. Rutledge grunted, pulling Shawn tighter to him, their chests flush against each other.

Looking into the dark eyes, Shawn moved. It was such a turn-on to see Rutledge's eyes slide half-shut, the way his head sort of arched back.

Shawn opened his legs a little bit more, adjusting his posture as he took it deep and sweet, the hot length of his teacher burning him from the inside out. He looked down between their bodies, fascinated by the movement of his own hips. He saw Rutledge's hands—big, and warm, and strong on his hips—direct the movement as he wanted it, guiding Shawn into riding him as Shawn's own cock stood untouched between them; it was red and thick, wetness glistening and sliding down its shaft.

Rutledge's thumbs stroked mindlessly at his hipbones, his tongue tracing a wet stripe on his neck as his cock stretched Shawn so damn good. Swallowing back his moans, Shawn pushed down to increase the pressure and to take him fully. The feeling of Rutledge's hard stomach sliding along the aching flesh of his cock made Shawn whimper, and he gripped Rutledge's shoulders a little bit tighter as he abandoned the rotations of his pelvis and started sliding up and down Rutledge's cock, hard and fast, wanting more, deeper, more.

Neither could breathe well and both needed everything harder and faster, and soon Rutledge was slamming his hips up to meet Shawn's on every thrust, and Shawn was gasping every time Rutledge hit his prostate, stars sparking behind his eyes. Rutledge was grunting, his muscles working as he lifted Shawn and lowered him down onto his cock, and fuck, his strength was such a turn-on, and Shawn wanted him, wanted him, wanted him.

Rutledge came first, and Shawn followed shortly after, jerking his way through his orgasm and sinking his teeth into Rutledge's shoulder to muffle his moans.

Shawn was only vaguely aware of Rutledge lifting him and laying him on his back: his eyelids grew heavy, his body languid with pleasure.

Just before he fell asleep, he realized they hadn't said a word to each other since Rutledge had entered the apartment.

Chapter Seventeen

Shawn woke up slowly, and the first thing he registered was a very naked and very warm body against his back. Rutledge.

They were spooning. Rutledge was spooning him.

Telling himself not to be silly—the bed was just very narrow, and there simply wasn't much space—Shawn opened his eyes, blinking groggily.

And found himself looking at two little girls staring at them curiously.

"Shawn's awake," Bee whispered, sucking on her thumb. "Can I be loud now?"

Emily shook her head. "Mr. Rutledge's still sleeping."

A tiny furrow appeared between Bee's brows. "But what is Mr. Rutledge doing in Shawn's bed?"

"He's sleeping, silly!" Emily said, forgetting to whisper.

Shawn felt the man behind him stir slightly and tighten his loose grip around Shawn's waist.

Rutledge mumbled something unintelligible, his lips brushing against Shawn's ear. Shawn grimaced and tugged the sheets higher, making sure the girls couldn't see anything they weren't supposed to see.

Bee pointed at Rutledge. "You told me to be quiet, but see, you woke him up!" She beamed. "Good morning, Mr. Rutledge!"

"Good morning," Rutledge said hoarsely right into Shawn's ear.

Goosebumps covered Shawn's skin. He squeezed his eyes shut and bit his lip. *Get a grip.*

"Morning," he said at last, turning his head.

It was weird to see Rutledge's hair so messy, but that, coupled with the dark stubble and all that naked skin, did strange things to Shawn's insides. Rutledge's dark eyes roamed over his face.

Shawn wasn't sure how to act. He wasn't sure where they stood.

"Why Mr. Rutledge slept in your bed?" Bee asked. "He doesn't have a bed?"

Rutledge's lips twisted. "Something like that, midget," he said, still looking at Shawn.

"Don't call her midget."

"I don't mind," Bee said. "I'm short!"

"She doesn't mind," Rutledge said.

Snorting, Shawn reached for his shorts and pulled them on, wincing a bit in discomfort.

"Sore?" Rutledge murmured, sitting up as well.

Shawn hopped off the bed and threw him a narrow-eyed look.

Rutledge's face was mostly inscrutable, but there

was a hint of something in his eyes…

"Drop the smug look," Shawn said and glanced at the clock on the wall. "Don't you have a class to teach soon?"

"Yes," Rutledge said, getting out of the bed. He looked so out of place in Shawn's tiny, shabby room it wasn't even funny.

Shawn turned away, grabbed the girls, and pulled them out of the room.

Don't be ridiculous, he told himself. It had just been sex. Yes, sex with another man—sex with his professor—but just sex. He had no reason to feel flustered. They were adults, they had wanted each other and they'd fucked to scratch the itch. Simple. Nothing complicated about it. It didn't have to be complicated.

Shawn was still telling himself that while he prepared breakfast for the kids when the doorbell rang.

He went to open the door.

"Good morning!" Mrs. Hawkins said, pushing past him. "Morning, girls."

"Good morning, Mrs. Hawk," the twins said in unison.

"Have they already eaten?" Mrs. Hawkins asked Shawn.

"No, I was just going to feed them, but I'm running a bit late and I'd really appreciate if you—"

She waved him off. "Of course, go take a shower. I'll do—"

Rutledge walked out of Shawn's bedroom, shrugging into his jacket. His hair was still wet after his shower.

Mrs. Hawkins stared. Then her gaze moved to Shawn.

Shawn felt a blush creep up his face. One didn't have to be a genius to guess what they had been doing last night.

Mrs. Hawkins's lips pursed into a line. Without a word, she nodded stiffly in Rutledge's direction, took the girls and ushered them into the kitchen.

Shawn blinked at her back. Just a few weeks ago, Mrs. Hawkins told him to live a little and get a girlfriend, but apparently this was a problem for her. What the hell. His sex life was none of her business.

"Find another babysitter for the children if you don't want them to grow up narrow-minded." Rutledge headed to the door. "I have to go. I need to change before work."

Shawn hesitated before following him to the door. Was it his imagination or was Rutledge really avoiding looking at him?

"Okay," Shawn said, forcing nonchalance into his voice. "See you around, I guess."

Rutledge went still before turning his head to him.

A beat passed.

Rutledge reached out, hooked his fingers in the waistband of Shawn's shorts, and pulled him close.

He bent his head and pressed his nose against the side of Shawn's neck before sucking hard on his skin. Shawn gasped from the mix of pain and pleasure.

In a blink of an eye, Rutledge was gone, and Shawn stared at the empty space he had occupied a moment ago.

What was that supposed to mean?

* * *

"Well?" Christian said when Shawn sat down next to him a few hours later.

Slumping in his seat, Shawn looked down at his hands on his stomach. "What?"

"Did you—you know?" The curiosity was clear in his friend's voice.

Shawn nodded. "Yeah," he murmured. "I fucked him again."

"So what now? You get over him?"

Shawn said, "Sure."

And then Rutledge entered the classroom.

As always, the hush was instant.

Rutledge walked to his desk, clad in a pristine three-piece dark suit that hugged his muscular frame. His strong jaw was clean-shaven—

"Yep, totally over him," Christian murmured.

Shawn flushed and averted his gaze. "I am."

"Sure you are. But wipe that drool off your face. Seriously, you're freaking me out. It's Rutledge. The guy is a total dick, he has no sense of humor, no heart—and he's not even handsome to compensate for his personality."

"He is handsome," Shawn muttered.

"He's not. All right, he has a great body and the confidence, but his nose is too big, and his eyes are cruel." Christian smirked. "Unless you're into that kind of thing, I guess."

Shawn rolled his eyes and accidentally caught Rutledge's gaze. Suddenly, Shawn could acutely feel the hickey hidden by his turtleneck, the bruises on his thighs, the soreness in his ass.

Rutledge looked away and cleared his throat.

* * *

"Look, he's come to pick Mila up again," Christian murmured, motioning with his head as they crossed the parking lot after their classes. "See, I'm not the only one who stares at him."

Shawn followed Christian's gaze.

Sure enough, there was a man leaning against a white Lexus, and yeah, he was attracting quite a bit of attention. The guy didn't even seem aware of all the staring students, looking bored and glancing at his watch from time to time.

"Damn, he's so gorgeous," Christian said.

Shawn eyed the guy critically. He really was rather startlingly handsome: tall and dark-haired, with strong, classically handsome features, a firm sensual mouth and striking deep-blue eyes.

Yeah, Shawn could understand why Christian was attracted to him, though the guy seemed Christian's complete opposite: all buttoned-up, serious and proper.

"I dunno, man," Shawn said. "He looks like he has a stick up his ass."

Christian wiggled his eyebrows. "Trust me, guys like that are usually the best in bed—kinky and intense." He sighed. "Damn, why are all the hot guys straight? It's so fucking unfair."

Shawn snorted and patted him on the shoulder. "At least you'll get to see him naked this weekend."

Christian grimaced. "Like a kid looking in the candy store window."

Shawn opened his mouth but shut it when a familiar black Mercedes stopped in front of them. The door opened.

"Get in," said Rutledge, without even glancing at him. He looked as though he was doing something very unpleasant.

"No, thanks, I'll take the bus," Shawn said.

"Get in," Rutledge said again.

Shawn glanced around. They were attracting quite a few curious looks. Shit.

He gave Christian a shrug and climbed into the car.

Rutledge slammed on the gas pedal.

"Are you crazy? Everyone saw us!"

Rutledge was silent, driving at a blinding speed.

"That's how nasty rumors start!"

Rutledge said nothing.

"Stop fucking ignoring me!"

Rutledge slammed his foot on the brakes.

Before Shawn knew it, Rutledge's lips were on his and his tongue was in his mouth.

Shawn moaned and kissed back, burying his hands in Rutledge's thick hair. Oh god, oh god, *god*.

Chapter Eighteen

The next few weeks flew by in a blur.

Every evening, Rutledge would come over and they would spend hours in bed, having sex until they were completely exhausted and fell asleep entangled in each other. Sometimes they would run into each other in the halls or Shawn would go to Rutledge's office and straddle his lap and they—

It was crazy. It was madness. Shawn couldn't keep his hands off him; it was like he couldn't control his body at all. He was weirded out by his own insatiable behavior; he'd never behaved like that before. This thing was actually getting worse. No matter how many times they fucked, no matter how many orgasms he'd had, he constantly wanted *more, more and more* of Derek but he couldn't get enough.

Derek.

That was another thing that bothered Shawn. Lately he had caught himself thinking of Rutledge as Derek far too often for his liking.

And to make things worse, Shawn wasn't all that sure it was just sex he wanted. He enjoyed kissing Rutledge way too much.

But the part after sex was the *worst*. Rutledge would kiss his face and his neck, softly and lazily, and Shawn would feel good, and warm—

Just like he was feeling at this moment as Rutledge nuzzled into the back of his neck.

"God, get out," Shawn groaned into the pillow, his voice still hoarse after the blowjob he'd given Rutledge earlier. "I have the night shift tonight. Need to be at work in less than two hours, and it'll take ages to get there." He grimaced at the thought. He hated the night shifts, he hated when he was sent to work at the restaurant on the other end of the city, and he hated leaving the twins with Mrs. Hawkins for the night.

Rutledge didn't move, his big body still sprawled over Shawn's back. He was too heavy and it was getting hard to breathe, but Shawn found that he didn't mind all that much.

"I need to get going, too," Rutledge said against his neck, kissing him there. "I have hundreds of papers to grade."

"Did you grade mine yet?"

"Yes."

"And?" Shawn's stomach tightened as he waited for Rutledge's response. He had put so much effort into it.

"It was acceptable," Rutledge said. "C."

Shawn deflated. "Oh."

Rutledge's lips stilled against his nape.

Then he rolled Shawn over and propped himself on his elbows above him. His dark eyes studied Shawn's face. "Are you… upset?"

"No," Shawn said lightly with a soft chuckle, averting his gaze. "I just… I just wanted to do better. To shut up the people who spread the rumors about us."

"If you got a better grade, it would have only made it worse."

"Maybe. But—I just really wanted to do better."

Rutledge gripped his chin with his fingers and forced Shawn to look at him. He had a strange expression on his face: irritation mixed with something else. "You did do better," he said gruffly. "I expected worse."

Shawn snorted, shaking his head. "Thanks. I guess."

Rutledge stared at him with the same vaguely irritated look before leaning down and kissing him.

Shawn wasn't entirely sure how they went from kissing to Rutledge's trying to push his cock into him—again.

"You've got to be kidding me," Shawn said, with a half laugh, half groan. "I'm sore."

"One more time," Rutledge said, managing to sound resigned and desperate at the same time. "I'll be gentle."

"That's what you said last time," Shawn said, but truth be told, he didn't mind at all. He was sore, but god, he wanted him.

"I was gentle," Rutledge said, his hips rocking gently into him. "Until you begged me to fuck you harder."

"I didn't."

Rutledge just snorted.

"Shut up," Shawn said, trying to keep his hips still—trying to hide from Rutledge how much he was enjoying the sensation of his cock deep inside him. He bit his lip to swallow back his moans. It was really embarrassing: Rutledge's cock wasn't even brushing his prostate, but he was loving the incredible fullness and the intoxicating intimacy of having another person—Derek—in him, on him, around him, Derek's heavy body pressing him down into the mattress, surrounding him…

"You don't have to go," Rutledge said into his ear, panting slightly as his hips rocked into him.

"What?" Shawn managed.

"You don't need to work there." A deep thrust. "I'll pay—"

"Don't even start."

"You accepted money before," Rutledge said, hitting his prostate, again and again.

"Don't." Shawn balled the sheets in his fists. It was too much. "Too sensitive." He tried to remember what they were talking about. "You know it was different before."

Rutledge's hips went still, making Shawn whine in frustration.

"How was that different?" Rutledge said in a strange voice.

Shawn blinked dazedly.

It was the first time they'd even remotely talked about this thing between them.

"I gave you blowjobs because I needed money," he said quietly. "I fuck you because I want it."

"It?"

"Because I want you."

Silence.

Shawn felt himself blush and told himself not to be silly. It wasn't like he'd said something Rutledge couldn't guess himself: it was blatantly obvious they wanted each other. But they had never actually said it.

"What?" he said, a bit defensively.

Making a low noise in his throat, Rutledge kissed him again and, changing the angle, set a steady, immensely satisfying rhythm.

"Good?" Rutledge asked hoarsely between his thrusts.

"Yeah." Shawn couldn't stop small moans from escaping his lips. "So good." His moans grew progressively louder with every thrust, his balls tightening as he approached orgasm.

"Yes, that's it," Rutledge said into his ear, kissing it. "Want you." He pressed wet, hot kisses all over Shawn's neck, his thrusts losing their rhythm but not losing any of their power. "Want you," he said again, his tone different.

A rush of pleasure hit Shawn hard, and he came with a groan, shaking with his entire body. God.

He was only vaguely aware of Rutledge thrusting into him for a while before he finally went still on top of him. Then, to his disappointment and relief, Rutledge pulled out and rolled off him.

Opening his eyes, Shawn turned his head.

Rutledge lay on his back, his eyes wide open. His face was flushed a little, his chest heaving, but he was far from being relaxed. There was a small frown on his face, his lips pressed into a thin line.

At last, Rutledge got out of the bed, got rid of the condom, and started dressing.

Shawn sat up, eyeing Rutledge's tense shoulders. "Can you give me a ride to work?"

Rutledge's hands stilled on the buttons of his shirt.

Shawn wasn't sure why he'd asked. He knew Rutledge's house was in a completely different part of the city. It just wasn't practical for him to give Shawn a ride if he had a lot of work waiting for him at home—he would waste hours if he did that.

Seriously, why had he asked? It was stupid.

Shawn stretched out his aching muscles, working out the kinks in his neck.

"Yes," Rutledge said tersely, looking away again. "Get dressed."

Shawn studied him for a moment. He got out of the bed and padded to him.

"It's okay if you don't want to," he said, buttoning the rest of the buttons on Rutledge's shirt.

Rutledge looked down at Shawn's fingers, his expression grim. "I want to."

Chapter Nineteen

Professor Bates was a dick.

At least that was what Shawn thought as the man ignored Shawn and continued walking.

"There's nothing to discuss, Wyatt," Bates said sharply, walking faster. "The assignment was due yesterday. I won't make an exception for you. It's your own fault. You're irresponsible! Thermodynamics is the most important branch of the science and you don't understand it. If you fail my class, which is looking increasingly likely, it will be deserved."

Shawn grimaced. Yeah, it really was his own fault. He shouldn't have spent so much time studying for his Fluid Mechanics paper, trying to impress Rutledge. He hadn't exactly impressed him, anyway.

"But—"

"Stop trying my patience, Wyatt," Bates snapped, shaking his head. "What's wrong with students these days?" And Bates started ranting about students' sense of self-entitlement, lack of focus, and lack of humility, looking more annoyed by the minute, and Shawn realized there was no way Bates would give him extra time to complete the assignment.

"Eric," came a familiar voice from behind them.

Shawn tensed and didn't look his way. Dammit. Rutledge was the last person he wanted to witness this.

"Is something the matter?" Rutledge said.

"This boy is lazy and irresponsible!" Bates said. "He doesn't do his assignments on time and now he asks me to give him a few more days! How is he going to be an engineer when he cannot even manage to pass the core courses?"

Shawn wanted the ground to swallow him up. Rutledge was the most intelligent man he'd ever met. He probably thought Shawn was dumb as a rock. Not that it mattered what he thought. Except it kind of did. It mattered. Too much.

"I was of the same opinion as you, Eric," Rutledge said, his voice indifferent. "But Wyatt has shown some improvement over the past few weeks. Give him a day. If he's late again, fail him."

Shawn's gaze snapped to him. There was no way in hell he could do it in one day.

"Good idea," Bates said. "One day, Wyatt."

"But—"

Bates glared at him. "One day."

Pursing his lips, Shawn nodded and left.

His feet brought him to Rutledge's office. The door was unlocked, and he let himself in.

Shawn leaned his hip against the desk and stuffed his hands into his pockets.

He didn't have to wait long.

Rutledge didn't look surprised to see him, but he seemed busy, carrying a stack of papers.

"You shouldn't have done it," Shawn said. "There's no way I can get it done by tomorrow."

"Why?" Rutledge put the papers on the desk and took his seat.

Shawn shrugged, looking at his boots. "I'm dumb."

"You're a scholarship student."

Shawn's lips twisted. "Yeah. I used to think I'm pretty smart, but… but I'm not. Most of the stuff Bates and you teach goes right over my head. One minute I think I understand thermodynamics, the next, I have no fucking clue what's happening. I really must be dumb." Shawn gripped the edge of the desk. "I feel like such a loser sometimes, you know? I can't find a decent-paying job, I can't buy the girls the things they need, and now this. I feel so useless—and stupid, and—I just—I just… Never mind."

There was a long silence.

He felt Rutledge's gaze on the back of his head.

"I'm no good at comforting people," Rutledge said, irritably.

Shawn turned to him and forced a small smile out. "It's okay. I'm surprised you haven't kicked me out yet."

Rutledge's lips thinned. He had a very sour expression on his face. "Come here."

Shawn had never moved so fast in his life.

He climbed into Rutledge's lap, put his head on his shoulder, and closed his eyes. Rutledge's strong arms tightened around him, and Shawn sighed in pleasure.

It felt so good. Just what he needed. It scared him—that he needed this—but he did. It almost felt better than sex.

"You're going soft, Professor," he murmured with a smile, breathing his scent in. It was familiar and oddly comforting.

"Shut up, Wyatt," Rutledge said, sounding even more annoyed, if that was possible.

Shawn brushed his lips against his neck. "Fine. You're very evil and nasty." He nuzzled into Derek's neck. "Five minutes. Then you can kick me out and we'll pretend it never happened."

Rutledge sighed. "Show me the assignment."

Shawn's mouth fell open. He lifted his head and stared at Rutledge. "Really?"

"I won't do it for you," Rutledge said, fixing him with a glare. "But I'll explain what you don't understand."

Shawn grinned and kissed him.

Chapter Twenty

Usually Shawn was a light sleeper.

But when the door to his room creaked open that night, Shawn had trouble waking up, his mind groggy. He burrowed deeper into Rutledge's warm shoulder, his hands tightening around Rutledge's arm.

The voices seemed to be coming from far away.

"Your brother is asleep," Rutledge said. "Go back to bed."

"But I had a bad dream! I'm scared. Shawn always hugs me when I'm scared!" It was Emily.

Shawn tried to open his eyes. It didn't work.

"Emily," Rutledge said sternly. "You're a smart little girl. You can't sleep with Shawn because the bed is too small for the three of us."

"I'll sleep with Shawn. You can go sleep with Bee!"

Rutledge chuckled. "I don't think I'll fit in your bed, midget."

Emily pondered it. "I can sleep on you. You're big, and Shawn likes to sleep on you."

Shawn certainly did, though he was disturbed that Emily knew that.

"You can't sleep on me."

"Why?"

"Because—because… Fine," Rutledge bit out at last, to Shawn's surprise.

Squealing in delight, Emily climbed onto the bed and onto Rutledge's chest.

"You're very warm," she said, yawning.

He really was. The room was very cold, but Derek was very warm. So warm.

"Sleep. And don't pee on me," Rutledge grumbled.

"I'm not a baby. I'm big. I don't pee in bed!"

"Good. Now sleep."

"You have funny hair on your chest. Shawn doesn't have funny hair on his chest. Why?"

That gave Rutledge pause. "Sleep."

"You don't like me," Emily mumbled. "You like Bee better."

A heavy sigh. "Why do you think I like her better?"

"You gave her chocolate yesterday!"

Shawn frowned. Huh?

"Because she asked. You have to ask if you want something."

"So if I ask, you'll give me anything? Anything, anything?"

"If I say yes, will you stop talking and sleep?"

"Yeah!"

"Fine. What do you want?"

"I want a puppy! Black and fluffy! With a white star on its forehead!"

A pause. "Choose something else."

"But you said anything!"

Shawn drifted back to sleep, still smiling.

* * *

"So," Christian said, leaning back and rocking in his chair a bit. "What's going on with you and Rutledge?"

Shawn looked up from his plate at him. "Huh?"

Christian laughed softly. "Come on. I'm not blind. It's been going on for weeks. I thought you'd get sick of him by now, but you still look totally fucked out most of the time—"

"I don't."

Christian gave him a flat look.

Pinching the bridge of his nose, Shawn admitted, "Yeah, all right. So what?"

Christian lifted his hands. "Hey, I'm not judging. Whatever floats your boat." He shrugged with a crooked smile. "It's none of my business if you have a crush on his dick."

Shawn slumped back in his chair and looked at Christian grimly. "It might be a bit more complicated than that." He ran a hand over his forehead, sighing. "I'm not even sure how to act around him in class anymore. It's like my brain stops working when he's around." He grimaced. "I kissed him yesterday outside his office. I couldn't help it. We were lucky it was late and no one saw us—I think."

Christian's eyebrows almost reached his hairline. He whistled. "Wait, are you, like, in a relationship?"

Shawn rubbed the corner of his eye. "No—I mean—I don't know. I… I kinda gave him a key to my place."

Christian started laughing.

Shawn kicked him under the table. "Shut up. It made sense to do it. Sometimes he comes very late, and I don't want him to wake up the kids with his knocking. It doesn't mean what you think it means."

"Oh, really?"

Shawn heaved a sigh. "I don't know. Things have been weird lately. He's so good to me sometimes, and I feel like… I feel so good with him, you know?" *Happy*. "It's so confusing."

"No shit. Don't you talk?"

Shawn shrugged. "Sure, we talk, but not about that. He comes to my place in the evening and if the kids are still up, it's not like we can talk properly. If they're in bed already, we don't spend much time talking." *I just want to get him naked and on me*. "And he's not exactly the talking type."

"Looks like he wants to talk this time." Christian nodded towards something behind him.

Shawn turned his head and saw Rutledge walking toward him briskly. Shawn stood and took a step away from the table just as Rutledge reached him.

"Something wrong?" Shawn murmured, glancing around.

They were attracting curious stares; instructors normally didn't come here.

Rutledge's shoulders relaxed a little. "No," he said, turning around and heading out of the cafeteria, clearly expecting Shaw to follow.

Rolling his eyes, Shawn did.

"I'm leaving for a few days," Rutledge said once they were outside.

"Where? Why?"

"It doesn't matter. It's none of your business."

Shawn crossed his arms over his chest. "Really? Then why are you even telling me?"

They glowered at each other.

Shawn refused to drop his gaze.

"I'm leaving," Rutledge said with finality.

"Fine. Go." Shawn bit the inside of his cheek, trying to hold back dozens of questions. Questions that would make him look like a pathetic, needy teenage girl.

Rutledge took a step to him; their faces were only inches apart now. There was a strange restlessness haunting Rutledge's dark eyes. Something was shifting between them, and it scared Shawn. And excited him.

A few seconds passed as they just looked at each other.

Some guy walked out of the cafeteria, and they sprang apart.

"Sir," the guy said respectfully to Rutledge.

"Right," Shawn said, shoving his hands into his pockets. "I'll go." *Before I jump on you and kiss you in front of everyone.*

Rutledge nodded stiffly and stalked away.

Shawn sighed. Dammit.

Maybe a few-days' break would do them good. Their relationship was getting too weird.

Or maybe the problem was it wasn't weird anymore.

Chapter Twenty-One

Rutledge didn't return in a few days.

Nor did he call. Shawn knew he could call, but the mere thought made him cringe. He didn't want to seem clingy.

By Friday, Shawn didn't know what to think. It didn't help that Emily and Bee kept asking where Mr. Rutledge was—the question Shawn had no answer for.

Where was he?

There was a niggling thought at the back of Shawn's mind that Rutledge was a commitment-phobe. Maybe he'd left because this thing between them freaked him out. If that was it, well, fuck him. Shawn would be damned if he let himself be the clingy one.

"What's wrong with you, man?" Christian asked on Friday morning as they took their seats in Rutledge's class.

"Nothing."

"You look like shit."

"Didn't sleep well," Shawn muttered, rubbing his eyes. It wasn't a lie. "I'm just—"

He cut himself off, noticing the professor who walked into the classroom.

It wasn't Rutledge.

His heart sank.

Professor Newland took the seat behind Rutledge's desk and smiled at the students.

"Good morning," the woman said cheerfully. "I'll be substituting for Professor Rutledge until further notice."

A cheer went through the room.

Shawn lifted his hand.

"Yes, Mr. Wyatt?" Newland said.

"Where is Professor Rutledge?"

She raised her eyebrows. "I don't think it's your concern, but if you must know… Professor Rutledge is absent due to family circumstances."

"Yeah," the girl sitting on Shawn's other side murmured. "I've seen in the news that he's marrying some politician's daughter."

Shawn stared at her numbly.

Christian put a hand on his shoulder and said something, but he could barely hear it.

Married? Derek?

"It can't be true," he whispered, more to himself than to the girl. "He's gay. And he's…" *Mine.*

Except he wasn't, was he? He didn't have any right to be angry. They were nothing to each other.

"Are you okay?" Christian said, looking at him with a frown.

"I'm fine."

"Shawn—"

"I'm fucking fine!" Shawn inhaled deeply and said, softer, "Sorry. I'm fine."

* * *

Shawn returned home early, dismissed the babysitter, sat on the couch, and watched the twins play.

Their dresses were worn out and too small for them. They needed new clothes.

He closed his eyes and thought of how much that would cost. Christmas wasn't far away, and Christmas was expensive, so he needed to save money. New clothes for the girls would have to wait until he found a better job.

Shawn sighed, rubbing his face. Yeah. That was what he needed to focus on. No more distractions. The kids depended on him.

The couch dipped as the girls suddenly climbed onto it.

"You're sad," Bee said.

"We don't like when you're sad," Emily said.

Shawn smiled brightly and wrapped his arms around them, pulling them close. They were warm and smelled of soap and sweets. Of innocence.

"No," he said. "Of course I'm not sad."

"When is Mr. Rutledge coming back?" Emily asked

once again, her blue eyes wide and glistening with tears. "He promised me a puppy! With a white star on its forehead."

Bee sucked on her thumb. "Yeah, when is he coming back?"

Shawn's heart clenched. At that moment, he hated Derek Rutledge more than anything. The girls had no one but Shawn; of course they'd become attached to Derek, since he had been practically living with them for the last couple of weeks.

Shawn smiled, but it felt like a grimace. "It doesn't look like he's coming back, sweetheart."

Emily's brows furrowed. "Why?"

How was he supposed to answer that?

Shawn averted his gaze. "Because he has his own family. And it seems his dad asked him to marry." At least that was the only explanation he could think of. "He's going to start a family now."

"Why?" Emily said.

Bee's lower lip trembled. "Why?"

Shawn looked between them and didn't know what to say.

"I don't know, baby," he murmured, pressing his lips to Bee's temple and pulling Emily closer. "I don't know."

Chapter Twenty-Two

Shawn woke up in the middle of the night, shivering.

He burrowed deeper under the covers. The room was cold and damp, as usual, but it was harder to ignore it after weeks of sharing body heat with another person. He missed being warm.

Shawn sighed, turned onto his stomach and hugged his pillow, angry with himself. This was getting out of hand. Enough. Fuck Rutledge and fuck his stupid warm body. Fuck him.

But no matter what he told himself, the ache in his stomach was still there. The hunger. The need that went beyond sex. He wanted Rutledge's body next to him, big and warm. He even wanted to hear his scathing remarks, feel his breath against his skin—

Shawn tensed and lifted his head. He could have sworn he heard voices coming from the living room. But the girls couldn't possibly be awake, right?

Frowning, Shawn climbed out of bed, shivering violently as the cold air hit his skin, and padded towards

the door. There was light in the living room, but it meant nothing: he had left the lamp on, because the twins were scared of the
dark.

Shawn opened the door quietly and froze.

Rutledge was sitting on the floor beside the girls' bed, one of the twins in his lap.

Shawn's heart started to thud in his chest.

He was back.

He was back.

"Where were you?" his sister said, rubbing her eyes sleepily with one hand while the other played with Rutledge's tie. It was Bee, Shawn decided. Rutledge seemed to have a bit of a soft spot for Bee, though it was strange that Rutledge was tolerating this even from Bee.

That was, until Shawn studied Rutledge's face. Even in the dim light of the lamp, his face looked uncharacteristically unguarded and tired.

"I was visiting my family," Rutledge murmured.

Bee sucked on her thumb. "I remember your family. Your dad didn't like us very much."

A strange look crossed Rutledge's face. He said nothing.

"Shawn said you're getting a new family."

Rutledge stiffened. "Did he?"

Bee nodded. "He was very sad."

Shawn felt himself flush. Did she have to tell him that?

Rutledge had an odd expression on his face. "Was he?" he murmured.

"I was sad, too," Bee said. "I don't understand.

Why do you want a new family? You have us."

Kids, Shawn thought, biting his lip. They had no fear. In some ways, kids were braver than adults.

Rutledge opened his mouth and then closed it. It was the first time Shawn had seen him at a loss for words. Rutledge's throat convulsed before he told Bee, "Don't worry, I won't be getting a new family."

Shawn breathed out.

"Aren't you supposed to be asleep, midget?"

Bee studied Rutledge seriously with her big blue eyes. "You're sad, too. Something bad happened?"

A humorless smile twisted Rutledge's lips. "You could say that."

"When I'm sad, Shawn hugs me and I don't feel so sad anymore. You want a hug?"

Shawn expected Rutledge to reject the offer with a sneer.

He didn't. He said nothing.

Taking his silence as a yes, Bee stood up and put her short arms around Rutledge's neck. Rutledge had to steady her.

Shawn stared at Rutledge's big hands on his little sister's back and then at his blank, stoic face.

Quietly, he closed the door and padded back to the bed.

About twenty minutes passed before he heard the door open again. There was a rustle of clothing before the mattress dipped under Rutledge's weight and he slid under the covers next to Shawn.

The speed with which Shawn latched onto him would have been embarrassing if Shawn could bring himself to care; he didn't. He just needed to kiss him. Needed to touch him. So he kissed him and Rutledge kissed him back just as hungrily, his lips urgent, almost desperate.

Shawn wasn't sure how many minutes they spent kissing—it felt like hours and seconds at the same time.

When they finally stopped kissing to breathe, Shawn was warm from head to toe. Hooking his leg over Rutledge's hip, he put his head on his chest. Rutledge's heart was beating under his ear, strong and fast.

For a long while, there was only companionable silence.

"He died, didn't he?" Shawn whispered at last.

He felt Rutledge go rigid under him. "Yes."

Shawn hesitated, unsure what to say. "What happened? Someone said you were getting married."

Rutledge sighed, something Shawn felt more than heard as Rutledge's chest expanded under his cheek. "It was Joseph's manipulations again. I went there because he told me he was on his deathbed. When I arrived, there was a huge gathering."

"What kind of gathering?" Shawn said, running his fingers through Derek's chest hair.

"Lots of politicians, rich businessmen and journalists. When I arrived, Joseph made an announcement."

Shawn's eyes widened.

"He actually announced your engagement without asking you? It's crazy."

He knew Derek's father was a despot, but that was ridiculous, even for him.

Rutledge seemed to hesitate. "I think… I think he hasn't been right in the head lately. And he probably hoped I wouldn't want to make a scene in front of so many influential people and journalists. He was right—our family would have become a laughing stock if I did that. I took him aside and told him if he didn't deny his announcement, I would do it myself." Rutledge paused. His voice was flat when he continued, "He got furious and had a heart attack. He was dead by the next morning."

Shawn closed his eyes. "Did you sort things out before he died?"

Rutledge chuckled, the sound harsh and humorless. "No. Even on his deathbed, he called me the biggest disappointment of his life. He tried to manipulate me even as he was struggling to breathe. Threatened to leave everything to Vivian's husband if I didn't marry that girl. Of course he didn't. He's—he was too old-fashioned for that."

Shawn's lips brushed the warm skin, and he breathed in, feeling the steady beat of Rutledge's heart against his cheek. "He's… I'm not saying that excuses him, but if he didn't care about you, he wouldn't have been… I mean, he's not a villain. When I talked to him, he was an arrogant asshole, but there was something he said… He said you were his son, and you were no fool. I think he's—he was just too proud to say anything nice, even if he felt differently, you know?"

Rutledge sighed. "It doesn't matter now. I don't care."

Liar.

Shawn nuzzled against his skin. “I’m glad you’re back, Derek.”

He felt Rutledge’s body stiffen for a moment and then relax against his. A strong arm wrapped around Shawn’s back and pulled him close tightly, almost bruising his ribs.

Shawn didn’t complain. He snuggled closer to Derek’s warmth and fell asleep momentarily.

He slept like a baby, for the first time in a week.

Chapter Twenty-Three

"Derek," Shawn said, closing the door.

Derek didn't look up from his computer. "Not now. I'm busy and you're... you're too distracting."

Shawn smiled. "Distracting, huh?"

Derek shot him a glare, but it was half-hearted at best.

"Come on, just tell me already!"

"No special treatment," Derek said. "You'll learn your grade when everyone else does. Tomorrow."

Leaning back against the door, Shawn bit his lip. "Did I fail?"

He wasn't sure. Derek had helped him a lot lately, explaining a lot of the stuff Shawn had missed at the beginning of the semester. Shawn had thought his understanding of the subject improved and that he'd done pretty well on the exam, but now, looking at Derek's grim face, he wasn't sure anymore.

"No," Derek said. "You didn't fail."

Shawn breathed out. "So what did I get? A C, right?"

Derek pursed his lips. "You got a B."

Shawn's mouth fell open. "Really? Wait, did you—"

"No, I didn't give you any special treatment," Derek said, his tone somewhat defensive. "You did a good job. You're not unintelligent. If you actually bothered to attend classes, you wouldn't have had any problems at all."

Shawn grinned, feeling stupidly warm and giddy. He took a step toward the desk, but Derek snapped, "Don't."

"Why?"

Derek fixed his eyes on the screen in front of him, his jaw clenched. "I told you. You're distracting. I have to work."

Shawn didn't want to go. He wanted to hug him. He wanted to kiss him. He wanted to celebrate with him. "But…"

Derek sighed through his teeth. "Fine. Come here and kiss me. One kiss. Then you will go."

Shawn went there and kissed him.

And kissed him again.

And again.

And one more time.

When their lips finally parted, Derek brushed his thumb over Shawn's cheek.

"Good job, Mr. Wyatt."

Shawn grinned and pecked him on the lips. "Thanks, Professor."

A reluctant smile appeared on Derek's face before he scowled and pushed him off his lap. "Now get out."

* * *

When Shawn opened his eyes the next morning, he found Derek watching him.

"Morning," Shawn murmured, their faces just inches away on the pillow. It felt unbearably intimate. "Sleep well?"

"No, I didn't," Derek said, his arm heavy on Shawn's back. "Your bed is terrible. I almost fell off twice."

Shawn smiled lazily. "No one's forcing you to sleep here."

Derek drew his lips into a thin line and averted his gaze for a moment before looking back. "It will be much more convenient if we use the bed in my house."

Shawn blinked. "You know I can't leave the kids on their own."

"I have a spare bedroom for them."

Shawn stared at him. "Are you asking me to move in with you?"

Derek's face was blank. "It would be convenient."

"Convenient?"

"Yes, convenient."

Pressing his lips together to keep himself from laughing, Shawn nodded solemnly. “Very convenient.”

“Shut up, Wyatt,” Derek said.

Shawn grinned slowly and looped his arms around Derek's neck.

They looked each other in the eye for a long moment, and Shawn felt something tighten in his chest. He said softly, “I love you, too, Derek.”

Derek stared at him for what felt like an eternity before he said, a little breathlessly, “Yes.”

Shawn laughed. “Okay, we’ll have to work on that—”

Derek shut him up with a kiss.

The End

Excerpt from *Just a Bit Obsessed*

Christian had seen some unlikely couples before, but nothing had ever come close to the affair between his best friend and Professor Rutledge. Except it wasn't even an affair anymore: Shawn had actually moved in with Rutledge, which was mind-boggling on so many levels Christian still had trouble believing it.

"Ashford," Rutledge greeted him, opening the door.

"Professor," Christian said awkwardly and entered the house. The man might be his best friend's lover, but there was no way in hell he could call Rutledge by his first name.

"Shawn is there," Rutledge gestured to the door to his left before giving Christian a hard look. "I'm working, so do not disturb me. Keep your voice down."

"Yes, sir," Christian said. What was it about this man that made him feel like he was three inches tall?

The door opened and Shawn's head emerged. "Are you bullying Christian again?" he said with an eye-roll.

Rutledge raised an eyebrow. "Me? Bullying?"

Giving him a long-suffering look, Shawn walked to Rutledge and kissed him. "Go work on your book while you still can. Don't forget that you promised Bee and Emily you'd take them shopping. They're super excited

—they've wanted a puppy for ages."

"Yes, black and fluffy," Rutledge said with a pinched expression on his face.

Shawn grinned. "And with a white star on its forehead! That's very important for Emily."

Rutledge gave him a glare. "What if there's no such puppy?"

"I'm sure you can bully people into finding you one," Shawn said. "Go work before they wake up."

Shaking his head and looking moderately irritated, Rutledge kissed Shawn on the lips and headed upstairs, presumably to his office.

"This is seriously creeping me out, man," Christian said, blinking.

Shawn snorted and led him into the room. "Sometimes it still weirds me out, too." He flopped down onto the couch and smiled widely. "But I've never been so happy."

Christian looked around the elegant room. "I bet it doesn't hurt that he's loaded, huh?"

Shawn just laughed. "So," he said, turning the TV off. "What's up with you lately?" He looked at Christian intently, his blue eyes serious. Those were some beautiful eyes, but they were light blue, not at all like—

Christian cringed. This was getting ridiculous.

"I mean, I've been a shitty friend lately," Shawn said with a sheepish look. "Things have been crazy, and Derek practically took over my life. I know it's a bad excuse, but—"

"Don't sweat it," Christian said, sinking into a comfy-looking armchair.

"So, what's up?" Shawn asked. "You've been kind of weird for a while."

Christian rubbed the corner of his left eye. "Remember the threesome I had with Mila and her boyfriend?"

Shawn nodded, but he was frowning. "Wasn't it a month ago?"

"Yeah," Christian said. "The thing is, it wasn't the only time it happened. Basically, it's been going on for a month—well, until Christmas."

Shawn's eyes widened slightly. "For so long? But you usually don't..."

"No, I usually don't," Christian said quietly.

There was a long silence, during which Christian found three screws on the ceiling and one small stain on the wall that might have been a bug at one time, though he couldn't imagine Rutledge smashing a bug.

"Are you in a relationship with them?" Shawn said, his voice slow and confused.

The laugh that left Christian's throat was a bit strained. "No. They're a couple, and I'm their fuck-toy. That's it."

"You aren't telling me something. I know you, Chris."

Christian looked at his hands.

"I don't want a threesome," he whispered.

"You mean..." Shawn sounded shocked.

"Yeah. I'm fucking jealous. And I hate it. It's driving me nuts."

"Jealous of whom? Him...or her?"

"Her," Christian said, his voice flat. "I hate watching her touch him, and kiss him—and fuck him." Christian chuckled. "I know; it's ridiculous. She has every right to touch him—she's been his girlfriend for two years. I'm nothing to him. But…"

"Are you in love with him?"

Christian licked his lips. "I—I don't know." He smiled humorlessly. "If this is love, it fucking sucks. I always thought love was supposed to make people happy. I've never felt so shitty before. It's not even just sex. I hate it when I see them together, when I watch them be all couple-y and cute.

She can touch him whenever she wants. She holds his hand. She spends nights with him—she lives with him."

He met Shawn's eyes. "I'm starting to hate her, you know. She doesn't deserve it. She's a fun, nice girl. I used to like her. And now I kinda want to claw her eyes out, stomp my foot like a kid and shout 'Mine!' every time she touches him. And I'm sure she already knows I want more of him. She wants me gone. I know that." Chris snorted. "And I can't say I blame her." He sighed heavily, running a hand over his face. "It's driving me nuts. And it's… it's fucking stupid. I barely know him. I don't understand him. But it's like… I can't separate sex from emotion, you know? I always could before, but with him, I just can't. I want to *please* him. Want him to like me. It's fucking ridiculous."

Shawn was silent for a while before asking quietly, "What about him? Do you think it's one-sided?"

Slumping back in the armchair, Christian sighed again. "I don't know. He's very hard to read. Sometimes I think there's something there, but… but I don't think he treats his girlfriend any different than he used to. He's always so attentive to her. Still the perfect boyfriend."

Shawn's mouth set in a grim line. "Don't shoot the messenger, but… if he felt the same way you do, wouldn't he be jealous of her, too? Their relationship would have deteriorated. If they're still fine, it… it doesn't really look good for you."

Christian's stomach churned. He knew Shawn was right. The same thought had occurred to him, too. "I know."

They both fell silent.

"What are you going to do?" Shawn said at last.

Christian bit the inside of his cheek.

"The smart thing," he said, meeting Shawn's eyes. "Quit while I still can."

About the Author

Alessandra Hazard is the author of the bestselling MM romance series *Straight Guys* and *Calluvia's Royalty*.

Visit Alessandra's website to learn more about her books: http://www.alessandrahazard.com/books/

To be notified when Alessandra's new books become available, you can subscribe to her mailing list: http://www.alessandrahazard.com/subscribe/

You can contact the author at her website or email her at author@alessandrahazard.com.

Made in United States
North Haven, CT
20 June 2024

53870944R00104